ALSO BY BEN FARTHING

Series: ***I Found Horror***

I Found a Circus Tent In the Woods Behind My House

I Found Puppets Living In My Apartment Walls

I Found a Lost Hallway in a Dying Mall

I Found the Boogeyman Under My Brother's Crib

Trilogy: ***Horror Lurks Beneath***

It Waits On the Top Floor

They Cling To the Hull

We Hide Our Faces

Standalone Books

The Piper's Graveyard

Those Who Dwell Below the Sidewalk

Crowded Chasms: Tales In Terrifying Places

I FOUND CHRISTMAS LIGHTS SLITHERING UP MY STREET

I FOUND HORROR

BEN FARTHING

For Arthur Rankin Jr. and Jules Bass.

"What's this? What's this?"

— JACK THE PUMPKIN KING, *THE NIGHTMARE BEFORE CHRISTMAS*

1

Right as I was about to admit that the snow was too cold and my gloves were too wet and I was ready to go home and join my parents in ignoring Christmas, I noticed a storm drain glowing.

It was red and purple except not red and not purple.

Pale gray clouds hid the late afternoon sun, blanketing this unfinished section of the neighborhood in a snowy dusk.

I'd been installing Christmas cheer onto a half-built house with decorations I'd begged from the more sympathetic neighbors and stolen from the less attentive ones.

It was just dark enough for me to notice the strange glow coming from the rectangular curb drain across the slush-covered street. I had stepped back from admiring how I'd wrapped a stolen strand of white incandescent bulbs around the porch railing when the glow from the drain caught my eye.

My friend David and his friend, Harold, were using my dad's duct tape to patch an inflatable Mickey Mouse in a Santa costume, halfway between the house and the sidewalk.

"Guys, look at that." I pointed across the street.

David's head popped up. He'd become sensitive to me and my family's grief since last Christmas. At first, his over-attentiveness embarrassed me, but now I was used to it.

Harold, on the other hand, had only moved in two months ago. He treated me like he treated anyone, which I would have appreciated if he wasn't such a jerk. He aggressively ripped off a piece of duct tape. It made a tearing noise.

"We could be at my house leveling up in Dragon Warrior," Harold complained, even though only one person could play at a time. "Instead we're fixing up broken Christmas junk for a broken house."

I ignored him to walk cautiously toward the glowing curb drain. Up the hill and up Pine Whisper Way—the neighborhood's main drag—the Foothill Pines Tacky Lights competition was in full swing. Bright lights of all colors shone throughout the snow-covered neighborhood. Down the hill, Pine Whisper Way passed through this last section of new houses. Their asphalt roofs and vinyl siding were completed, but their insides were as empty as the almost-repaired blow-up Mickey.

These eight unfinished houses connected the living, breathing part of Foothill Pines above with an actual pine forest below. That's where my house hid. We'd been here before the neighborhood.

"The house isn't broken, stupid-ass." David took the tape from Harold and covered the last rip in Mickey's side. "They're not done building this part, yet."

I approached the hole in the curb with its strange glow. A gust of wind blew icy snowflakes into my eyes. Below, light flickered from left to right.

I heard Harold kick Mickey. "'Stupid-ass' isn't a word. It's 'dumb-ass,' you dumbass." He lowered his voice, but kept it loud enough that we all knew I could hear him. "And your weirdo friend is a dumbass for wanting to decorate a house where no one lives."

Packed-down snow on the street proved a slippery walkway, but I made it across.

The argument behind me faded into the periphery of my perception.

Chilly wind whispered past my numb ears. I crouched by the glowing drain.

I decided that "flickering" hadn't been the right word for how the light moved. "Wiggling" was better. That not-red and not-purple light *wiggled* across the back of the cement catch basin, projected by something down below, out of my sight.

This cement box under the sidewalk was where snowmelt drain pipes intersected. It was five feet tall, a fact I knew because I'd been inside plenty of times. I was small for an 11-year-old, which meant that when we played in the drainpipes beneath the sidewalks, I could slide straight into these rectangular storm drains, while David and Harold had to go down into the gulch to enter through the four-foot concrete pipe that spilled into a creek.

I knelt down on the road. Snow dampened and chilled my knees.

Indefinable colors grabbed tightly ahold of my attention. I wanted to get in there, feel them across my skin. I imagined they'd feel more like Christmas than any of the tacky lights up Pine Whisper Way.

And even though my parents were ignoring the holiday, I really wanted it to feel like Christmas again.

As I leaned in, Harold's mocking laugh interrupted me. "Now this is a real dumbass move. What are you doing, Douglas?"

I got down on my belly to stick my head into the storm drain.

This time, David interjected. "For real, are you going in there?"

I turned my head to the side and scooted forward. "There's some kind of light."

The cement opening scraped at my cheekbones. I wouldn't be able to climb into the sewer this way much longer.

"What sort of light? Can you see what it is?" David's plastic bag-covered sneakers patted through the snow and then he was crouched down next to me. If there was a mystery to be solved, David was into it. He'd read and watched *Harriet the Spy* a thousand times and his mom had a shelf full of old *Encyclopedia Brown* paperbacks. Supposedly that was how she'd learned English.

Harold whined behind us. "Guys, it's cold as balls out here. Let's go play Dragon Warrior at my house. Or we could do Street Fighter, if you agree not to pick a bitch character."

I didn't give two shits about Harold's Nintendo games. Right now, I wanted to know what those lights felt like, and why I suddenly smelled a relaxing aroma of a freshly cut Fraser Fir Christmas tree. That's the kind Mama always used to make Dad find.

We didn't have a tree this year.

"We can even watch Rudolf like you guys wanted to," offered Harold, "I'll watch a stupid kids movie with you if we can just go inside."

I'd missed out on watching that this year, along with all the other stop-motion classics that Mama used to get excited about every December.

But something about these lights, just out of sight, felt like the bright simplicity of Rudolf and Chris Kringle and the Snow Miser.

I inched farther into the drain, trying to see what was casting the light.

During the spring and summer, inside the catch basin, snowmelt from the mountains above would enter from the bigger pipe and then run down to the gulch and into the creek. From there, it went out of the neighborhood, past my house, and to the river.

But on Christmas Eve, the sewer was dry.

I scooted forward. My eyes passed over the ledge but my chin still stopped me from turning my head.

Straining to look down, in the corner of my vision I saw little pinpricks of alternating not-red and not-purple, moving across the bottom of the basin in a line. It clicked what they were: lights on a wire strand. Christmas lights, getting dragged from the downhill pipe, across the damp cement floor, and into the uphill pipe.

Both the moving lights and the scratching sound they made on the cement reminded me of the M&Ms-candy-themed model train set that my father didn't set up this year.

"What do you see?" Excitement filled David's voice, but he couldn't get his head inside. "Should I run down into the gulch? Are we going inside?"

I closed my eyes. I listened to the clickety-clacking of Dad's model train. I sniffed in the sap smell of Mama's Fraser Fir.

"Douglas? Can you see what it is?" David sounded anxious.

I reluctantly opened my eyes and answered him. "There's a light strand getting pulled through the pipes." I shimmied forward another few inches. My chin passed over the ledge and I could turn my head to look down.

Seeing it straight on was even stranger.

Three green wires emerged from the downhill pipe at a slow but steady rate. They each had not-red and not-purple light bulbs every twelve inches. I couldn't tell if they were incandescent or the new brighter LED bulbs.

Their glow was unfamiliar in a way I couldn't put my finger on. One of the strands turned across the catch basin to enter a pipe that went under the street. The other two went into the uphill pipe toward the occupied section of Foothill Pines.

Harold spoke closer than I expected. “Douglas, are you waving a flashlight around down there?"

I didn't flinch at his disbelief. It didn’t matter right now.

David spoke up for me. “Bend your boney ass over and look in the drain yourself. The lights are crazy. They’re all over the place."

I watched the strands slither through the drainpipes. "They're coming from downhill."

"It's only your house down there." Harold laughed. "I thought your family stopped celebrating Christmas."

That was a kick in the balls, but I let it go. I had an idea that might change Christmas for me this year. “Hand me that tape.”

I crawled out from the drain. The front of my pants chilled my legs. Snow clung to my coat.

David gave me the roll of duct tape.

I unrolled a long stretch but didn’t rip it off. Then I tossed the roll into the drain and held tight to the end of the tape. I crawled back inside to look down.

“Are you fishing it out?” David asked. “Shouldn’t we investigate where it’s coming from, first?”

I didn’t care. Finding this light felt like a Christmas miracle and I wanted it to fill me up.

I dangled the tape roll, like one of those claw games at

the miniature golf place in town. I touched it against the moving wires until a bulb wedged in between the roll and the tape itself. "Got it!" This must be what David felt when he scored a winning goal on the school's soccer team.

Carefully, I pulled the roll up, hand over hand.

Wire bunched up in the catch basin as it continued to feed out from the downhill pipe, but couldn't get past where I'd snagged it.

It surprised me that the moving wire wasn't being pulled from uphill, but rather pushed from downhill.

Another three gentle pulls and I had the strand of Christmas lights in my hands.

The green coating around the wires felt almost too malleable. Pressure pushed against my hand as the wires continued to bunch up below.

The lights this close to my face left a taste of frosted sugar cookies on my tongue.

I crawled back out, displaying my prize: a loop of weirdly-colored Christmas lights.

"What are you gonna do with that?" Harold scoffed.

David asked the same question, but with more concern. "Something's weird about them. What are they doing down there? What color is that?"

He squeezed the wire between his thumb and forefinger. "It's kinda like when you pick a dandelion. You know how if you roll it back and forth, it'll come apart into little strings? We definitely need to figure out where it's coming from. That'll tell us why it's so weird."

I snatched the wire away from him. It scraped against

the edge of the drain where both ends of it disappeared. "Don't tear it apart. I need it."

I didn't care where it came from. It was an answer to my prayers to Santa. I deserved to listen to "I Want a Hippopotamus For Christmas" and taste candy canes and feel the wrapping paper shudder as I ripped it away from a big box I'd been eyeing under the tree all month. I was going to have the Christmas that my parents didn't want anymore. This light was the key, even if I couldn't quite wrap my mind around *how* it was the key.

I dragged the lights toward my adopted Tacky Lights house. The drain eagerly gave me more slack.

"You can't leave these across the road," Harold protested.

"It's fine," I said. "I'm going to decorate this house."

I reached the front porch and wrapped the folded wire around the banister.

Plans poured into my head. I could feed this wire all over the house until it covered every shingle, every piece of siding, every window. Until the house was a blinding beacon that would convert any Christmas skeptic.

I would go get Mama and Dad and my big reveal of my own decorations would make them love Christmas again. Maybe not this year, but it would at least plant the seed.

Then I heard Mama calling me home for dinner. I couldn't ignore her.

2

I COULDN'T IGNORE MAMA, but first, I had to plug in my original lights.

I dropped the strand that I'd pulled from the drain—I'd run out of time, so my original display would have to do.

We grabbed the extension cord and together dragged it two houses uphill to Harold's place. His was the first occupied lot on the street after the unfinished section. We plugged it in on his front porch and then turned to admire our handiwork.

White lights lit up in an irregular spiral around the porch railings. Colored lights outlined two windows and had little tails down to the ground. My patched-up Mickey Mouse's blower motor buzzed and he unfolded himself to raise a candy cane high.

Altogether, it wasn't much, especially compared to the rest of Foothill Pines, but it might be enough.

I'd been hoping that I could show Mama and Dad after I was done. Then they would finally see... something. I couldn't quite articulate what I wanted the result to be. I knew I wanted them to like Christmas again.

But now, with the not-red and not-purple strand of lights leading from the porch steps to the drain across the street, my project felt *off*.

I didn't get it. Just a minute ago, those weird lights had helped me remember all the amazing parts of Christmas.

Mama yelled again.

"She sounds worried," David said. "You better go."

He didn't have to say out loud, *she's anxious about what happened last Christmas Eve.*

We said goodbye and "merry Christmas," and David reminded me that I was invited to *Noche Buena* with his family tonight after dinner, but I reminded him that tonight I was finally going to show my parents our festive handiwork.

Harold unplugged the lights.

"Hey! I need those."

"What are you doing that for?" David demanded.

"So he doesn't waste my electricity," Harold said.

"You don't pay the bills," David said. "You're just being a jerk."

My anger had flared up but I stuffed it back down. I was empty. I needed to be empty. "It's fine. I'll run and plug them back in right before I show my parents."

"If you're sure that'll work," David said. "But Harold's still being a dick."

We parted ways. Harold went inside, David started his trek uphill into the beautiful gauntlet of tacky lights displays, and I aimed myself downhill, on a path that would take me past my hopeful house and the strange lights, then into the darkness that led home.

I walked between the first pair of empty houses. They stared down at me with dark window eyes.

The buzz of Mickey's blower interrupted what might otherwise have been a peaceful winter scene.

My boots scraped on the salt and slush of the pavement. Messy, but less slippery than walking on the packed-down snow on the sidewalks.

Far down the hill, through the trees, a yellow glow burned faintly—my parents' porch light. Outside of the Christmas holiday, it would have been a bright beacon marking home. But when the tacky lights Contest started, Dad stretched out a canvas tarp over the side of the porch so Mama didn't have to see Christmas.

It wasn't like I could get lost on the straight shot home, but not having that beacon made the dark around me stretch on forever.

Wind chilled my wet clothes. I had a lonely walk ahead of me. I shivered.

As I approached the looped strand of lights crossing the street, its two colors twisted together in my vision. Suddenly, it felt like a very bad idea to step directly over it.

So instead, I walked over to the sidewalk. I'd rather be careful on the slippery packed down snow then get back close to those weird lights.

I was passing the drain where the wires emerged when I heard a soft, wordless song.

I stopped walking. Without the crunching of the frozen snow beneath my boots, I heard the melody more clearly. Its higher pitch rung out over the low rumbling of Mickey's blower.

Someone was singing a wordless rendition of *Silent Night*. Someone inside the catch basin beneath my feet.

The eeriness of the situation crept through my wet clothes to embrace me like the December breeze.

I wanted to run all the way home to Mama—who cared how slippery it was?

But also, I liked *Silent Night*. Dad used to hum it to Erica while he rocked her to sleep and I lay awake in my bed. After he laid her down, he'd rub my back until he finished the carol. This December, he'd only hummed that George Straight song about crossing your heart.

The night chill dulled as I closed my eyes to see Dad singing Christmas carols as he tucked me in. I'd secretly wished for that every night since Thanksgiving, but listening to this singing coming from the drain was even better.

I opened my eyes. Of course it wasn't better. What a stupid thought. A dumbass thought.

The singing strained over Mickey's blower.

It still had the allure of the Christmas I wanted for my family, but now I could hear what David had seen in the lights. Something not quite right, just out of range of my perception.

Swallowing my fear, I stepped down off the sidewalk to look into the storm drain.

Four costumed carolers stood in the catch basin.

I could only see them from the eyes up. Two men wore old-timey top hats. One had wrinkles on his forehead and white eyebrows. The other was no older than my dad. Two women wore bonnets. Like the men, one had gray hair and the other was younger.

Warbling color played against their faces as the light strand I'd dragged out shone next to them.

I stepped back.

Their pupils were too pale. Green and blue and brown, but colored like I was seeing them through frosted glass.

The shape of their faces—the top half in view—had that same wrongness that I couldn't quite put my finger on.

And when had they gotten in there? I'd been reaching inside just a few minute ago.

They felt dangerous. I had to get away before their song wove its dark magic into a snare.

The carolers leaned toward me, stretched upward toward the basin's ceiling.

Their noses came into view and then their chins.

They had no mouths.

Skin stretched and folded as they worked their jaws with song.

I fled for home, falling only once.

3

I DASHED UP MY DRIVEWAY.

Frozen gravel busted apart.

Dad's truck was parked next to Mama's sedan. I took the porch steps in big leaps. Once I'd put Dad's canvas barrier between me and the weird lights up the hill, I finally felt safe.

I flung open the front door. Our house was a four-bedroom, one-bath built during that strange time when the number of bedrooms was more important than usable space.

Mama was pulling a Tombstone pizza out of the oven. Dad had the *Andy Griffith Show* on VHS playing on the living room TV. *Rudolph the Red-Nosed Reindeer* was about to come on TV, but I didn't expect him to switch over.

They both turned to look at me as I crashed through the door, out of breath.

Everything that had just happened wanted to burst out

of me. I needed my parents to tell me I'd be okay. But they thought I'd been inside at David's house. I couldn't tell them I'd been decorating a house for Christmas. Not yet. That moment still needed to be perfect.

We'd drive into town to see the big tree in front of the library. Then on the way back, I'd tell them I wanted to show them something up the hill, and they'd see the house that *I* had decorated, and then they'd realize... then they'd realize it.

I needed this to happen more than I needed defrosted pepperoni pizza. And I loved those little cubes of Tombstone pepperoni.

Those carolers in the storm drain might have been the scariest thing I'd ever seen, but they were up the hill now. It's easy to shrug off the impossible when you're eleven. Tonight was my last chance to reclaim Christmas. If it didn't happen this year, it never would. That's what mattered right now.

It was time to ask Mama and Dad to go out together.

"Guys?" I began.

Mama silenced me with a stern look.

It deflated my determination.

She dropped the pizza pan on the stove with a clatter. The oven door slammed shut. "I called you five minutes ago. What took you so long?"

"I was finishing something with David. Sorry, Mom." When I thought of Mama I called her *Mama* in my mind. I went back to doing that after last Christmas Eve because Erica had still called her Mama. I was keeping Erica alive in my head and I was showing Mama that she still had a little kid to take care of, even if I was eleven now. Except, of course, I wasn't showing her anything, because I only called her Mama inside my own head. Out loud, I called her *Mom* like I had since I was six. That was my plan until I found a way to share memories with Mama without her excusing herself to the bedroom and shutting her creaking door and falling onto her creaking bed and crying for an hour.

The pizza cutter *slinked* as Mama sliced dinner into triangles. "It's cold out there tonight. I want you warm in bed early."

She wasn't even going to acknowledge that it was Christmas Eve.

My plan tried to rise up inside me again but there was so much weight holding it down.

A whistled song played from the TV, meaning that Dad's *Andy Griffith* episode was over. He leaned sideways over his chair. "I thought you were playing at David's house and then coming straight home. Did you dally outside? You look pale."

All I had to do was say, *Let's go into town*, and then everything else would happen naturally, and we'd have Christmas again.

But I only said, "No sir. I came straight home."

Mama mixed up a pitcher of Koolaid. "Set the table, please."

I did as I was told.

Last year, and every year I can remember before that,

we'd eaten cinnamon bread and peaches for Christmas Eve dinner. Then we hung up our stockings along the bookshelf—dad wanted a crackling fire in the fireplace and was paranoid about house fires. Mama would say, "You can open one present tonight." It was always pajamas that she'd sewn herself.

Tonight would be my first Christmas Eve going to bed in old pajamas. In fact, I didn't have any clean ones, but I didn't dare mention pajamas to my parents tonight.

Erica had been wearing her Christmas Eve pajamas when they finally found her frozen body.

I don't know why she left the house. When I'd been in second grade, I'd been afraid to even leave my bed in fear that Santa Claus would pass us by. Maybe she wanted to catch a glimpse of the sleigh and reindeer atop the roof. Mama and Dad think she wanted one more look at the tacky lights up the hill. They never said that but they don't have to. Erica loved looking at the lights. Christmas Eve after we read the second chapter of Luke and watched Charlie Brown and unwrapped our new pajamas, Erica had wanted to walk up the hill again. Mama and Dad said no.

Erica was always stubborn.

Even though we weren't technically part of the neighborhood, everyone in Foothill Pines was out looking for my little sister. All the cops and firefighters from in town were trudging through the snow with spotlights.

David's dad, Mr. Perez, found Erica. She was in her pajamas with her *Toy Story* blanket wrapped around her shoulders. No coat and no boots because she'd snuck out her bedroom window.

Nobody told me the details, but I pieced together bits and pieces I overheard from Mama and Dad and from David's parents. They found Erica stuck up to her knees in snow and mud in the empty lots where the unfinished houses now stood. I don't know why she wasn't on the sidewalk.

The search took eighty-seven minutes. Dad walked up that sidewalk at least three times. He was within twenty feet of her. But the snow was falling fast and so Mr. Perez only found Erica through the blind luck of tripping over her.

That's when most of me stopped existing. When I became empty.

Now I was the kid from the bottom of the hill whose sister died even though the neighborhood came together to help. I stopped being the kid whose family waved to everyone on their Sunday morning walks. I stopped being the kid whose family hosted cookouts for their neighbors up the hill.

I couldn't even be the kid who ran around with David and pretended we were space explorers.

I was only *Douglas, who lost his little sister just last year, and I don't think his parents are taking it well but can you blame them?*

I used to tell myself that Mama and Dad still saw me. That they knew I wasn't empty. But I stopped believing that lie after Thanksgiving.

So at the kitchen table, as I ate my Tombstone pepperoni pizza in silence, I couldn't insist aloud that *I* had hopes and plans for this Christmas season, if we could just go out together for a little while.

I finished my pizza.

If I wasn't having a Christmas Eve with my family, then I'd have *Noche Buena* with David's family. "I'm going to play Mario and go to bed," I lied to my parents.

I walked to my room.

Maybe the only thing I wanted from my parents seeing the decorated house was to get out of *this* house on *this* night.

Erica left a Christmas-shaped wound in our family.

When Dad got home from the morgue Christmas afternoon, Mama was still sitting on the floor next to the tree. Her cheeks were puffy with tears and exhaustion. She held Erica's wrapped presents. The wrapping paper was red with cartoon depictions of Timon and Pumba.

I sat in Dad's recliner. I'd already tried hugging Mama and telling her I loved her. Her quiet sobs of, "Not now, honey," should have been the first sign that the season of wonder was over in the Evans household.

Dad's Ford Taurus rumbled into the driveway, its failing transmission making an audible lurch as it shifted into park. He walked inside, gave me a look of disappointment that I wasn't consoling my mother, and then he went to her side. He stood and examined the ornaments while Mom leaned her head on his blue jeans.

Dad thumbed a popsicle snowman ornament. He must

have thought that Erica made it, but I did. I remembered gluing it together in kindergarten. Five years later, Erica had that same kindergarten teacher, but that Christmas they made popsicle reindeer.

I sat quietly. My own grief felt like a twister that started in my gut and was pushing its way up my throat, while filling my limbs with the urge to move.

I jammed it all down.

"Open your presents, Douglas."

At first, I didn't understand Dad's words. They might as well have been Japanese, as well as they fit into our current situation. I recognized each word individually, but together they didn't make sense.

Dad couldn't possibly have meant, "Open your presents," and so I tried to figure out what I'd really heard.

Mom sniffed. "Go ahead, honey. Your father worked overtime for a month to get you just what you wanted."

A sour fist grabbed hold of the twister inside me. Dad had bought me a Nintendo 64. I'd begged and pleaded. I'd convinced Erica that SHE wanted a Nintendo 64 so that she'd join me in begging and pleading. But I knew it was a long shot. It was four times the normal price range of what Santa brought.

But that's all Mom could have meant.

I opened my gift thirteen hours after the doctors pronounced Erica dead. I traded it in at *Software, Etc.* a week later. The credit got me a Super Nintendo. Lame compared to the new 3D games, but it was one step removed from that Christmas gift which I never wanted to see again.

You'd think, with that personal experience, I would have seen coming what happened this December.

But I didn't.

I didn't blur together my grief with Christmas like Mama and Dad did. I helped Dad put away his O Gauge model train, and helped Mama put away her Department 56 Snow Village porcelain houses, and it hurt. I put the ornaments away while Dad wrapped up the string lights, then we carried the dead Frasier Fir out into the woods and tossed it down into the gulch.

I didn't feel like these things were permanently ruined, only that they'd failed to do their magic this year. Maybe next year, when the house felt a little less empty, and I was crying less frequently, we could try again. The train whistle might sound more like Christmas the next time around.

I had a hard time in January.

In February, when the snow was still on the ground and every inch of the house sparked vivid memories of Erica, I started looking forward to next Christmas. Her death had first interfered with our lives by destroying the holiday, so if we could just make it to next year, things would reset.

When spring came in late April, I remembered playing in the woods with Erica, splashing through the snowmelt puddles, and picking new buds off the rhododendrons to throw at each other. Walking home from David's house one afternoon, taking the trail through the woods that goes past the gaping cement pipe sticking out the hill, I missed Erica extra hard. I sat on a rock by the stream and cried so many tears. The only thing that got me back on my feet was thinking that at the end of the year, Christmas would come again and we'd decorate and get each other gifts and we'd learn how to do it all just the three of us. Then things would be okay again.

At the end of the school year, early July, Mrs. Kite brought me in front of the class. Three other sixth grade teachers came in, too. They handed me a card with cupid on the front, which I later realized was supposed to be a baby angel. They told me I was so brave for finishing out the school year strong despite my great loss. Mrs. Kite refused to make eye contact with the other teachers while she told me that Erica was in heaven now, waiting to play with her big brother again. Nobody in class talked to me the rest of the day. Even David didn't say anything until we were on the bus.

Only the part of me that had lost Erica existed. That's all anybody saw. The rest of me was empty.

I made my Halloween costume with David—and Harold, he'd moved in by that point. We went Trick-or-Treating up and down the hill and in and out of the cul-de-sacs. When I got home, I proudly showed off my haul to Mom and Dad. Dad's smile had a sad hue to it. He told me to give a bag of M&M's to my mother. She said she'd rather have an Almond Joy, which wasn't funny but still we laughed.

It was after Halloween when I started getting ready for Christmas. It was finally on its way.

I went up to the attic to slide the boxes of ornaments right next to the ladder. I snuck down the light strands that we used on the tree and made sure all the bulbs were still lit, before I put them back in their place. When Dad was at work, I went out to the garage and polished up the model train tracks so electricity would pass freely into the locomotive's wheels.

This was the part of me that had gone missing—that Erica had taken with her. It's why adults acted like all that was left of me was how much I missed my little sister. But now, Christmas would come and bring all the other parts of me back. Me and Mama and Dad would get ready for the Christmas season and we'd figure out how to remake our home.

We drove to Denver for Thanksgiving with my Mom's parents. My excitement to get home and start the Christmas season had me bouncing and babbling and making dumb jokes, to the point that Grandpa laughed about how happy of a kid I was, and I must be bringing an extra special light into our home. On the drive back, all I could think about was getting a new tree, setting up the train and village, and hanging my ornaments. I wanted to put up Erica's, too. I hadn't told Mama that, yet, but I was sure she'd let me at least put up the construction paper Santa with Erica's kindergarten photo glued onto its face.

It was still early evening when we pulled into the driveway. We wouldn't actually start decorating tonight—we never did—but we'd bring everything down from the attic and in from the garage to get a bright and early start in the morning.

I kicked off my boots and ran to the hallway, ready to open the attic door.

But instead, Mama poured me a bowl of cereal, told me I could watch whatever movie I wanted but she had a headache and would be going to be early. Dad went with her and they shut their door behind them.

My house felt really empty.

It was the Saturday night after Thanksgiving, but instead of prepping to decorate for Christmas, I was standing next to a bowl of Frosted Flakes, alone.

I waited for them to come back and realize they'd forgotten what day it was.

It was the first I'd considered that they hadn't been looking forward to Christmas as our big family reset. They didn't want it to come at all.

When someone dies, grief is a twister trapped in a glass jar.

When you realize that you died too, that jar breaks.

When Mama and Dad clicked their lamp off and the light under their bedroom door went black, it made my stomach ache like I was about to blow chunks.

A heavy realization of loss came next and it came on slow.

Not only had I not been granted my wish of a new start with my family, but I was also losing even the normal parts of Christmas.

Every December, Dad would quietly wave me into his bedroom to proudly show off the gift he'd picked out for Mama. And I always knew when he was about to do it, because there'd be a smile stuck on his face and he'd have *Jingle Bell Rock* stuck in his head and forcing its way out despite the fact that he only knew a handful of the words.

Sometimes in December we'd get off the bus and run inside to see Mama sitting in her easy chair, embroidery hoop untouched in her lap, eyes softly watching the blinking lights on the tree. Usually, Mama had to be knitting or crocheting or stitching new knees into my jeans in order to relax. It was only at Christmastime that I regularly found her sitting happily, doing nothing.

Erica was stubborn from the day she was born—that's what Mama said. She refused to eat anything except Dino Nuggets and Kraft Macaroni and Cheese. When Mama bought the Food Lion brand she had to hide the box or Erica would squeeze her lips so tight together you couldn't pry them open with a crowbar. Erica always wanted to play with whatever toy I had out and she'd scream if I didn't give it to her.

But some days during December, Erica would eat Dad's famous chili poured over a baked potato. Some days, Erica would leave me alone with my Legos to instead gather all the ornaments from the tree that she could reach. Not every day, but always some days.

At school, my teachers had more sing-song in their voices. My classmates got jittery but picked on me less. David talked nonstop about the new Nintendo game he wanted, or new Nerf gun, or new Goosebumps book. It was only one gift for him, which I thought was weird until I got older and understood that my family was poor but not *poor* poor.

And of course, the Foothill Pines Tacky Lights Contest lit up the hill above our house. No matter who the judges picked, everyone cheered and said congratulations and promised to come back bigger and brighter next year.

Christmas was the one time of year when everyone had a reason to be happy for no reason.

But Mom and Dad weren't letting it in the house.

The part of me that loved Christmas—which was a *big* part of me—couldn't exist anymore.

But it wanted so badly to exist.

That's why I'd been out there decorating one of the unfinished houses in the bottom section of Foothill Pines.

It's why I'd wanted to work up the nerve to ask Dad and Mama if we could drive into town to see the huge Christmas tree in front of the library. Tonight was the last night it would be lit, and that's something we always did, the four of us. It could still be something that the three of us did, and then I'd show them the house that *I* decorated, and then they'd realize… what?

How the *Christmas* part of me wasn't empty.

Then we'd come back home and decorate quick as we could. Maybe even in time for me to sit between them on the couch and watch the end of *Rudolph*.

But I couldn't work up the nerve to ask them to go to

the library tree. Getting in the car and driving into town was too much.

But what I could do, was insist that they walk with me outside and to the edge of the woods. From there, they could see the lights that I'd hung, and then they'd see.

First, because Harold was a dick, I had to go run and plug them back in.

I devised a plan. I set my TV's alarm function to switch on in thirty minutes. I turned the volume all the way up and switched it off. I left a note on my bed: *Walk up to the neighborhood. I want to show you something.*

Mama would get stressed out that I was gone like Erica had been last Christmas Eve. So I wrote *good* at the end. *Show you something* good.

I got my old coat and boots out of my closet, and then I went out the window to get my tacky light display ready to remind Mama and Dad about Christmas.

4

WALKING through the dark woods didn't scare me anymore.

As I approached the tree line, the Christmas lights up the hill became even brighter than I expected. They shone between the bare lower trunks of the pine trees.

I left the woods and reached the start of the sidewalk.

I couldn't make sense of what I was seeing up the hill.

The eight unfinished houses glowed with a thousand pinpricks of eerie light: not red and not purple.

Light strands ran along the corners of the houses and their roofs' ridge lines. They outlined the porches. There was no landscaping in front of the houses yet—no bushes—but even still, bunches of string lights sat on the snowy ground in front of the first floor windows.

All the lights were alternating not-red and not-purple.

Between each house, the lights were connected by two drooping strands. As I traced the wires from house to house, I knew what I was going to find at the end. The strings led to the house that I'd decorated with my friends. But even while the lights I'd hung were powerless and dark, these not-red and not-purple string lights climbed up the edges of my adopted house to outline the roof and chimney.

Across the front yard, past the deflated Mickey Mouse, that eerie string of lights led over the snow, down the curb, across the street, and into the drain.

If I stood very still, I could almost see the line of lights slithering ever so slowly, feeding into the patterns it had created. The glow on the houses themselves shifted continually as the wires and bulbs all moved in a big loop.

Wind blew past my ears. I wanted to know if those weird Victorian Christmas carolers were still inside the drain. If they were still missing their mouths. But from down here at the bottom of the hill, I couldn't see inside.

I listened for their wordless singing. All I heard was the wind, or was the melody of "Away in a Manger" hiding behind that whistling gust?

It sent chills down my back, the idea of seeing them again.

Still, I had to plug in my lights so I could show Mama and Dad.

But could I bring myself to walk between the rows of newly-decorated, empty houses?

What was going on?

Was this because *I* had pulled them from the sewer?

I didn't like dwelling on any of those thoughts.

I didn't want to figure out why some weirdos had been singing in the sewer, or why I'd convinced myself they didn't have mouths. They were just regular carolers.

I wanted to have Christmas. I was going to show Mama and Dad my lights and nothing was going to stop me.

My old boots squeezed my feet. My coat wasn't nearly warm enough, but it did block the wind. The only thing comfortable were my ears, beneath the knitted hat.

It only took a minute to reach the first house.

Closer up, I was sure that, yes, the light strands were moving. They crawled along the corners, outlined the windows, and wrapped around the chimneys. Staring at them too long made my head buzz. The red bulbs teased the color red, but weren't quite there. The purple bulbs shined more sharply, emitting their light in little daggers.

I felt pinpricks in my eyes.

I squeezed them shut and shook my head. When I opened them again, the strange feeling was gone.

I picked up my pace.

As I neared the light strands that crossed the street to the storm drain, I expected to hear those weird carolers again. Out here alone, it was harder to convince myself that they'd had mouths. I'd seen what I'd seen. Their vocalized music had been muffled by unbroken skin.

I paused to listen. Whispering wind. The low buzzing of motors up the hill, keeping inflatables inflated. And fainter, barely there over the competing sounds: singing.

Four-part harmonizing of "What Child Is This?"

Slowly, like in a nightmare, I turned my head to look into the drain.

Empty.

That not-purple and not-red light glowed from within, and the looped strand that I'd pulled out still pushed outward to feed the houses, but the carolers had abandoned their post.

I felt vulnerable. I scanned all the yards around me, looking for the source of the singing.

The eerie houses in my immediate vicinity had empty yards, except for the trail of lights and the deflated mouse. Up the hill, where the properly-colored tacky lights contest was going on, my neighbors' yards were more festive. Wicker reindeer woven with white lights. Blow molds of Santa, elves, candy canes, and the baby Jesus. I saw an inflatable Grinch, Frosty, and even the skeletal Pumpkin King in a Santa hat. Harold's neighbors on the uphill side had even filled their front yard with plastic trees below a banner that read, "Christmas Tree Farm."

Somewhere hiding in all this holiday spirit were those carolers.

I scanned the neighborhood as quickly and thoroughly as I could, but there were too many obstacles. Wind interwove itself too intricately with the carolers' song, so I couldn't pinpoint its source.

David would love this mystery. It'd scare the hell out of him, but he'd be so excited to uncover where the carolers were hiding.

Not me. This wasn't exciting.

Part of me said I should run back home.

But that part was a dumbass.

Once I plugged in my display, I could show Mama and Dad. And then I'd salvage this Christmas and set us up to have a better one next year, and one even better the year after that.

I trudged ahead.

Those sewer lights crossed my path. I avoided looking directly at the light, not only to avoid seeing their creeping movement, but also because the colors were starting to hurt my eyes.

Keeping them in the lower periphery of my vision, I drew close.

A scent of hot chocolate teased me.

I couldn't focus on the weirdness. That would be a reason not to show Mama and Dad my light display.

I hopped over the wire. I set my sights on Harold's front porch, where my extension cord led.

His family's decorations were scant, despite Harold's insistence that they had a shot at winning first place the very first year they'd lived in Foothill Pines. His parents were on a cruise, which struck me as strange. His grandma had come to stay with him. Her ancient Subaru Forester sat in their driveway, its dark green paint a strong contrast to the snow on the roof and hood.

The wind gusted and I pulled my jacket collar tighter around my neck.

I was almost there, then I could sprint home.

Mr. Brink's front porch, directly across from Harold's

house, came into view. His holly bushes had blocked my line of sight before.

The four carolers stood on his front steps, their backs to me. The two women wore brown dresses under thick coats. Bonnets covered their heads. The two men wore knee-length pea coats and black top hats. One had gray hair, the other black.

I froze, terrified that they would turn around and catch me out in the open of the empty street.

They transitioned from "What Child Is This?" to "God Rest Ye Merry Gentlemen," in four-part, wordless harmony.

When they'd been in the drain, their song had evoked Christmas memories. Now the noise felt like sandpaper rubbing my skin.

Mr. Brink hadn't opened up, so the carolers sang to a closed door.

I wondered if their voices scraped at the wood, scratching their way inside.

Again, the urge to run home almost overtook me. Mama and Dad could protect me from whatever I'd pulled up from the storm drain.

But all I had to do was run up Harold's front walk, onto his porch, and plug in the lights.

I could do it.

I hurried, careful to avoid stepping loud enough to catch the carolers' attention.

When I reached his top step, the door opened a crack.

A warm yellow glowed from within, juxtaposed with the shadowy, pale white of the snow all around.

I heard Harold's yelled whisper. "Douglas! Get inside before they see you." He stuck his head through and waved me in.

Harold quietly shut the door behind us. He peered behind the curtain of the window next to the door. "They did something to Mr. Brink. Did you see it?"

5

In the two months since he'd moved in, I'd never seen Harold scared. At least, I'd never seen him scared without trying to hide it.

He opened the curtain and pointed across the street. "See that reindeer?"

With the foyer light behind me and the evening darkness outside, I had to lean in close to the glass to see past my reflection. The carolers stood with their backs to us, in a semicircle around Mr. Brink's open door.

Had it been open before?

The carolers blocked my view. I couldn't tell whether Mr. Brink was standing there listening to them.

It would only be him. He had no family.

"Look at the reindeer," Harold whispered.

I found the decoration in Mr. Brink's yard. It was uphill from a holly bush, where I hadn't seen it before.

The reindeer's wire mesh legs were as thick as telephone poles. Its body had swollen to the size of a full grown bull. Its head and antlers had grown disproportionately to the point of looking like a bobble head. And all over, where earlier there'd been bright white LED lights, now those not-red and not-purple lights from the sewer had woven themselves all throughout.

Lights blinked from inside Mr. Brink's open front door —those same two impossible colors.

Was this my fault? I'd pulled the lights from the sewer because I wanted to fill myself with those Christmas memories that they had evoked. Now I didn't know what was going on.

"That's Mr. Brink," Harold said.

"Where?" I tried to see past the carolers and inside.

"The reindeer. I looked out the window because they wouldn't stop singing—it was so loud I thought they were at my house. But they were crowding up on Mr. Brink's porch."

I asked, "Did you see their faces?"

Harold continued as if I hadn't spoken, lost in recounting his story. "I didn't have a real good view inside his door, but these lights were flashing funky colors. Mr. Brink ran outside—he had to push between the weirdly dressed people. He tripped over that white reindeer decoration. Knocked the whole thing down."

"Stop," I said. I didn't want to hear the next part. It was Christmas Eve. Everything was supposed to start getting better tonight.

"Mr. Brink didn't get up. The reindeer did. I mean, it

fell over and then grew up sideways. And now it's not right. Look at it. It's all thick and bumpy and its head is way big."

The strangeness of what he was claiming pulled me away from my wallowing. "It *grew*?"

"Those people just kept singing. They didn't even turn around when Mr. Brink pushed through them."

"Harold," I said. "Answer me. The reindeer got bigger?"

He looked down at me, remembering I was there. "Like a tree in fast-foward. That's not even the original reindeer. Nobody set it back up. I think it's still lying on its side inside this new big one."

"With Mr. Brink," I added. I pictured him trapped inside the wire-mesh decoration, touching those irritating lights.

"Yeah. He's probably in there." Harold closed the curtain. "What do we do?"

Why was he asking me? I'd never hung out with him without David. Since David was independently both of our friends, he became the de facto leader. I wasn't ready to decide how to react to our neighbor getting swallowed by a mutated wire reindeer.

We should get some garden shears and go to the drain. Snip, snap, and all the weird lights get cut off.

But I didn't say that out loud. I wasn't in the habit of sharing my ideas with anyone but David. No one wanted to hear what I thought, unless it was about missing Erica.

"I don't know," I finally said.

"That's fine," Harold answered. "I called David. He

likes figuring stuff out. He'll be here in a minute and he'll know what to do."

I grew more frustrated. Tonight wasn't the night for David to meticulously solve a mystery.

I didn't want to solve a mystery. I recognize that it's selfish, but in that moment, I didn't even want to help Mr. Brink get out of there.

I only wanted to plug in my lights and then show them to Mama and Dad.

"Can't we just wait for them to leave?" I asked. "Maybe they'll go back into the sewer and we'll never see them again."

"They came from the sewer?"

Oh right. Harold didn't know that.

Of course he didn't—I hadn't told anybody. "The carolers were in the drain. I saw them on my way home."

"Then they're connected to the lights. David will figure out what that connection means. Here's what we'll do. We'll keep an eye out for David so he doesn't get caught out there with the carolers. But if they come over here first, we'll go hide in my parents' room. That's where my grandma is staying while they're gone."

I remembered when my parents room felt like a safe haven.

Harold peeked behind the curtain. His cheeks went pale. He took an unconscious step back. His jaw dropped enough for his lips to part slightly.

"Mouths," was all he said.

I looked out the window.

The four carolers strode across the street toward Harold's front walk. The women clutched fuzzy hand warmers. The men carried green hymnals. All of their jaws worked with song, muffled only slightly by the skin where their mouths should be. That skin stretched and contracted with the melody of "In the Bleak Midwinter."

I yanked shut the curtains. That snapped Harold out of his terror. "Come on, my grandma's upstairs. We'll call the police from up there."

But when we turned around, Mrs. Bancroft was already coming down. Her gray hair bounced in pink curlers She held her nightgown tightly around her chest. "I heard carolers. Are you boys going to let them in?"

Harold raised his arms wide to block the door. "Don't! There's something wrong with them." He opened the curtain. "Look at their mouths!"

Mrs. Bancroft squinted as she reached the bottom of the stairs. "All I see is my own reflection."

I backed away into the living room. This was a debate within a family that wasn't mine. No better time to not exist.

"That's some unpleasant singing," Mrs. Bancroft said.

"I'm telling you, Grandma, they're not regular carolers. They did something to Mr. Brink!"

I eyed my escape route through their living room, out the back door. Harold's Christmas tree was between his empty fireplace and his TV. Beneath the tree was a pile of wrapped presents. Two stockings hung over the fireplace, one with Harold's name, one with "Grandma." On the TV, Rudolph the Red Nosed Reindeer lowered his antlers at the Abominable Snowman.

Even with his parents out of town, Harold had been ready to have a perfect Christmas.

Behind me, the singing grew louder and the argument continued.

"They took over Mr. Brink's house and now they're over here. What do we do?"

If I fled out back right now, even if I made my way home, I couldn't bring my parents back out to see my decorations. I hadn't even plugged them in. Something terrible was happening in Foothill Pines and it was preempting my one shot at making Mama and Dad remember Christmas.

And here's the stupidest thing I did that night. The most dumbass thing.

For a moment, I managed to convince myself that nothing outside was wrong. Because if that were true, I could have the night I'd planned.

I'm not saying it makes sense. I'm only saying that in that moment, I wanted to show my parents my decorations so badly that one last time I pretended everything was fine.

Mrs. Bancroft turned to look at me. "It's Douglas, right? Do you know what my grandson is so worked up over?"

I shrugged.

Maybe if I'd been honest, things in Harold's house would have happened differently.

Mrs. Bancroft gently pushed Harold aside. She unbolted and opened the front door.

Eerie singing flooded in like a muddy sludge.

I knew I'd made a terrible mistake.

Harold grabbed his grandma's hand and fruitlessly pulled at her.

I couldn't see out the door, but I could see Mrs. Bancroft's eyebrows furl in confusion as she saw the mouthless carolers.

The wood floor of the foyer lit up with spots of not-red and not-purple.

The strange lights were beneath the house.

I stepped toward the back door, toward my path home. But I couldn't leave Harold, even if he was a jerk.

I dashed back across the room, keeping Harold's grandma between me and the carolers. I grabbed Harold's hand—already wet with sweat.

"Come on. We can't stay here."

Harold turned back to his grandma. "Shut the door."

Mrs. Bancroft had gone ramrod stiff.

She was transfixed by the carolers mouthless faces, frozen by fear.

"Grandma, please," Harold begged.

As I reached for Harold again, my movement gave me a line of sight around the old woman to see the gray-bearded caroler with the blank skin between his mustache and chin. His eyes locked with mine. They widened with excitement. It reminded me of last December when mom and Erica had got home from Christmas shopping and Erica wanted to tell me what my gift was but she was old enough now to understand the concept of surprise.

It was that same eagerness that I saw on the caroler's face. It scared me deeper than anything else so far that night.

I turned to flee.

Patches of living room carpet glowed in those impossible colors.

In my cowardice, I hopscotched through the lights to the back kitchen door. In my periphery, I noticed the TV. Rudolf was pressed up against the inside of the screen, his nose turned from bright, cheerful red, into the grating color of the sewer lights.

I flung the back door open to icy wind and I froze.

Starlight reflected off the snowy backyard slope down to the trees. Snow covered the roof of a green shed and the crossbar of an unused swing set.

The carolers' wordless song wrapped around the house to reach me back here. I pulled my hat tight over my ears.

I nearly leapt down the steps into the yard, until I suddenly remembered we had complete cloud cover. There could be no starlight reflections in the snow. I made myself slow down to look where I'd been about to leap.

The light was coming from beneath the snow. And it wasn't the pale white of stars. The snow in Harold's backyard glowed in penny-sized dots of not-red and not-purple.

It was a minefield, with space between the dots that could just barely fit my too-small boots.

Slowing down had allowed space for guilt to seep in. I turned back to see if Harold and his grandma were following me.

I saw through their kitchen, into the living room. The rooms were awash with shifting colored lights, although the kitchen table and chairs cast flickering shadows on the ceiling.

I called for Harold.

Had it already happened?

What he claimed he saw happen to Mr. Brink—had Harold and his grandma already collided with their own Christmas decorations? I imagined Harold sinking into the branches and needles of their tree until the green points absorbed his body. I imagined Mrs. Bancroft struggling to free him, only to get her feet caught in the pile of presents below while the boxes unwrapped themselves to drag her within.

Instead, Harold came into view, trying to run but dragged by his own insistence on tugging along his grandma behind him.

His feet fell on a dot of light.

My heart skipped a beat.

But Harold and Mrs. Bancroft kept on running.

"Boys, is this some kind of prank?" Despite her question, Mrs. Bancroft kept following her grandson.

They came out onto the deck with me.

"Run over to the neighbors'," she said. "I'm coming, too. We'll call the police."

Harold looked around the yard. "How'd they get under the snow? Is this all because you pulled them out of the sewer?"

Mrs. Bancroft looked over her shoulder back through the kitchen. “Go on, now, boys. Let’s not stay here.”

Harold took a step down but I stopped him.

“Wait, I’m looking for a good path through.” Festive chicken pox infected the yard but I thought I saw a path with enough space between the lights. “Let’s go.”

The song behind us grew louder.

Mrs. Bancroft leaned to see back into the house. “Are they inside? We didn’t invite them in.”

I led the way, hopping down the steps. The path I’d mapped hooked deeper into the yard before cutting back over to the side of the neighbor’s house, where the lights hadn’t penetrated the snow yet.

"Where are you going?" The old woman asked. "This way is fastest."

Harold shouted protest, but she was already walking straight across the yard. Her slippered foot stepped right onto an eerily glowing patch of snow.

A string of not-red and not-purple Christmas lights whipped up out of the snow to wrap around her legs. She let out a surprised, “oh!” and fell onto her hands.

“Ow,” Harold’s grandma whined. The snow cushioned the worst of her fall, but she reached back for her tangled legs. “What is that?”

Harold ran to help. He tugged at the strands of lights.

Fear of what would happen next froze my boots to the ground.

“Douglas! Help me get this off of her.”

That woke me back up. I ran to her side, still careful to avoid stepping on the lights under the snow.

"What did you leave out here, Harold?" she demanded.

"I don't know!"

Harold and I tugged at the wires. Their green casing had too much give, like it was made of Silly Putty. It vibrated with unnatural energy. My hand got too close to a lightbulb and it made a sizzling noise.

I couldn't budge the light strands at all. "Do you have scissors inside?"

Harold still tried to dig his fingers between the wires and his grandma's legs. "The carolers are still in there."

Faster than it fell from the sky, snow gathered in little drifts against Mrs. Bancroft's bathrobe.

I brushed it away, insisting that the strange phenomenon not be real.

It didn't feel like snow. It felt like stringy cotton balls, the sort of fake stuff that sat around Santa's chair at the mall. But it was still cold.

It accumulated more and more until it was one long drift that circled her entirely, like a police chalk outline.

"Something weird is happening," I said. "You have to get up."

She moaned in pain. "I'm trying. Get these lights off of me."

The chilly cotton fluff rose above her feet and calves, burying them. I backed way, not wanting to put my hands underneath the fake snow.

Harold tried brushing it off. "What is this stuff?"

The light strands suddenly pulled even tighter. The old woman let out a surprised yelp of pain. Her legs started digging into the ground.

The powder piled up over top of her legs, her hips, her back. She craned her neck backward to hold her head above the snow. It made me think of Erica "swimming" in our bathtub, her little brunette curls dangling into the bubbles.

Mrs. Bancroft said her grandson's name, pleadingly. "Harold."

She collapsed into a pile of cottontail snow. Air rushed in to fill the space where her body had been, sending a puff of cotton upward against the flurries and sounding a little "pop."

My gut backflipped.

Harold screamed.

He dug at the snow where she'd been—real snow, now. He kept screaming. He dug through the light top layer of snow, down through the packed-down frozen layers beneath. His fingertips were bright red. Still he screamed, although the sound was taking on a lilting, melodic wobble.

It wasn't him. The sound was coming from behind me. The back door was open, the yellow kitchen light spilling onto the porch. The carolers' song bulged outward from inside. They were making their way through the house, drawing closer.

I grabbed Harold around the wrists. Two of his fingernails were bleeding.

"She's not under there," I yelled.

I led him away from the hole he'd dug, carefully stepping over the glowing patches of snow, until we reached the safe ground of the paved driveway next door.

"We have to warn the neighbors," I said, but Harold wasn't listening. He was staring into his own front yard, terrified at what he saw.

6

A FEW MINUTES BEFORE, I'd run up Harold's front walk past a single wire candy cane light and a handful of white lights around the porch. Now, strings of not-red and not-purple lights covered Harold's house, vining up the walls and over the roof like invasive kudzu. Most of the bulbs were a normal size—the size of my pinky nail—but I spotted one bulb outshining the others in both size and brilliance. It clung to its wire above Harold's front door. Within its not-purple glow, an eyeball floated.

It made me think of Jurassic Park, with the mosquitoes trapped in amber.

Another oversized bulb hung below Harold's bedroom window. Inside the glass was a pink, plastic hair curler.

I looked to Harold, hoping he didn't see what I did, or at least that he wasn't making the connection between the curler and his grandma.

But he stood at my side, eyes widening in growing fear. He pointed to the front porch.

Another large bulb dangled from the porch roof. It gave off a headache-inducing violet light and it contained inside it lips and a tongue. Rather than float lifelessly, the bottom lip opened and closed, silently weeping in pain.

I don't know if Harold read his grandma's lips screaming "help me," but I did.

"What is that?" Harold stammered.

"I don't know," I answered honestly. What did this mean? Had the lights sucked her underground and then sliced her into her component parts? Had they used her as a pattern to make something new?

Although my mind was pulled to these questions, it was David—not me—who would know how to investigate them.

I only wanted to get away.

The carolers' song grew louder behind the house. They were following us.

"Is that Grandma?" Harold asked, still captured by the contents of the giant lightbulbs.

As much as Harold had been a jerk since he'd moved in, I couldn't leave him standing there like a mannequin waiting for a steamroller. I jumped in front of Harold to look him in the eyes. "We have to run."

"She's in pieces."

"We don't know what's going on. But we have to get out of here." I looked at his house again. I saw movement inside the window. It looked like a canine shape, bent over and walking behind the curtains. But with horns.

A reindeer. There was something strange about its movement. Something jerky in the way the shadow behind the curtain hopped and pranced.

Harold finally snapped out of his trance. "Where do we go?"

I looked at him and then back to the window. The reindeer silhouette was gone.

Down the street to my house, more light strands now crossed over the slushy pavement and slippery sidewalks between the unfinished houses. It'd be a maze to get through without touching the wires. "Your neighbors," I said, "we'll get them to call the police."

I looked uphill and suddenly saw the dozens of families whose Christmas was about to become like mine. Not just the Jones family right next door with the fake Christmas tree farm, but everybody on the school bus with me, everybody who'd waved as me and David ran up and down the street, everybody who'd left their warm homes a year ago to look for Erica.

Even as my concern for them grew, it was accompanied by frustration that all this was stealing the Christmas Eve I'd been planning since the Saturday night after Thanksgiving.

"I wish my dad were here," Harold said.

I wanted mine, too, but help from your Dad was for people who weren't empty.

"Oh God, my dad!" Harold breathed heavy. "Grandma's

his mom! What's he gonna say? He's gonna blame me for not keeping her safe."

"It'll be okay."

We couldn't cut across the neighbor's yard—the "Tree Farm" of fake Christmas trees was too dense. It felt like a good place to get slowed down and caught by the carolers.

Instead, I led Harold by the hand to the sidewalk so we could go down the walkway in the middle of their yard.

We found David running down the slippery sidewalk in coat and jeans. No plastic bags over his sneakers this time. He was out of breath. His eyebrows raised in surprise. "What are you doing here, Douglas?"

His older sister Maria came behind him. She looked annoyed. "You snuck out for this? I thought you were going to do something fun."

"I told you, Harold said he needed help."

Maria rolled her eyes but didn't leave.

Now that David was here, I felt more confident. "I came up to plug in my lights. I found all this." I waved generally behind me.

"The carolers got my Grandma," Harold told David. "But you can figure out how to undo it, right? You can be a detective like in your books."

"What carolers? Why are you acting all weird? Are you making fun of Douglas again?"

"We'll explain in a second. The carolers are coming—can't you hear them? We've got to warn the Jones." I led Harold, David, and a very confused Maria up the Jones' front walk, between the two halves of their plastic tree farm.

They were in the running to win the tacky lights contest. They had string lights on every corner of their house and had spelled out "X-MAS" on their roof. Their bushes were covered in netted lights. But their real show-stopper was that they'd set up fake trees in the rest of the yard to make it look like a tree farm fully decked out for Christmas.

We ran up their recently-shoveled front walk. With the decorated plastic trees on either side, it felt like running through a movie version of the North Pole.

For a moment, I considered sitting down and losing myself in the Christmas that I'd missed out on.

But Erica had sat down last year.

I ran to the front porch and banged on the door. Harold lingered at the bottom of the steps.

A moment later, an old man opened the door. Mr. Jones. I knew they had adult kids, but I didn't know why they weren't visiting this year.

Another thing I didn't know, was how the hell to convince them they had to run away from their house.

"The carolers don't have mouths," I said. "They're coming here next. Can you call the police?"

The curious look on Mr. Jones' face turned to concern. "What'd you say?"

"Lights grew up out of the ground. I saw them in the storm drain this afternoon but now they're all over the new houses and they killed Harold's grandma. Look." I stepped back and pointed down the street, wanting him to see how all the unfinished houses had grown decorations in the last hour.

He scrunched up his face in irritation. Mrs. Jones joined him in the doorway, wearing a bright green sweater with a white snowflake knitted on the chest. "Young man, why aren't you home?"

I shouldn't be the one talking. David was better at this stuff. But he didn't know what was going on.

"Do you hear that singing?" I asked. "They're coming here right now. You need to run."

Mr. Jones put his arm around his wife, more for his comfort than for hers. "You want us to run away from Christmas carolers?"

"Look at them. They don't have mouths." I turned to point at the carolers who I could hear approaching up the sidewalk. But the fake forest blocked our view. I could only see straight out from the house, up the front walk, between the bright and colorful plastic trees.

Maria cut in. "I'm sorry, Mrs. Jones. I think this prank got out of hand."

I shushed her.

Mrs. Jones noticed Harold. "Harold, what are you doing out here? Do your parents know you're out playing pranks?"

As much as I wanted to help these people, I wasn't going to be here when the carolers arrived. "When they get close, you'll see they don't have mouths, but they're still singing. And string lights will start coming out of the ground. You have to run when that happens. They got Harold's grandma. And Mr. Brink."

I pointed, but again, the plastic trees blocked our view of it.

"Listen, boys," Mr. Jones said. "Run on home and wait for Santa. Save the pranks for next Halloween."

I gave up. I turned to run for the street.

The carolers stepped into view, blocking the exit from the fake tree farm.

The four carolers moved as one. The wind rustled the old woman's hair and I thought for a moment that the skin on her forehead moved in the wind, as well.

"Holy shit," David breathed.

Harold shrieked. He ran up the porch steps but Mr. Jones blocked him from hiding inside.

"Hey there, go on back to your own house. They're just caroling. Do I need to have a chat with your parents?"

Maria went ramrod stiff. "Is this part of your prank?"

"Come on." I looked for a way past the carolers.

Walking four abreast, the outer two brushed tree branches with their elbows. We were walled in.

"David?" I asked. "What do we do?"

But he still hadn't found his bearings.

I darted into the plastic pine tree farm, my friends following close behind.

7

PLASTIC PINE NEEDLES walled me in and scratched at my face.

Strings of incandescent bulbs wrapped around each tree—blues, greens, yellows, oranges, reds, and purples. Red glass ball ornaments hung from the branches, reflecting the tiny lights.

"These lights are normal," Harold whined, "right?"

They were, but the not-red and not-purple light strands creeping up the fake tree trunks were not.

"What do you mean, *normal*?" David asked.

Maria tried to push her way to the front, but we were moving too quickly. "Are you sure this is the right way?"

"Every way's the right way, dumbass," David said. "It's a small front yard."

Except we'd been running thirty seconds or more. That was plenty of time to make it out of the Jones' yard.

"Hey, don't talk to me like that, you little shit," Maria

retorted. "Guys, slow down. Who were those people singing?"

I didn't want to run the show but I couldn't let David's sister slow us down while we were stuck in a forest being overrun by those strange lights.

"Harold," I asked, "can't you see over the trees? How close are we?"

"I'm not that tall." Harold stretched to his toes but the star tree-toppers were still three feet above his head.

Harold was five-foot-eight. These had all been five-and-a-half-foot trees earlier.

I looked at the sky, walled in by plastic pine needles nearly as high as a basketball net. How had that happened?

"This way." Maria pushed ahead of me. "Once we get home, I'm telling Papa that you snuck out. And called me a dumbass."

"I'm helping my friends," David shot back, but followed his sister.

I fell in line. A lightbulb brushed my cheek. It was abnormally hot.

Harold yelled. "Hey! This isn't normal. I was taller than these trees this morning."

"You were ten minutes ago," I added. "We need to get out. Quick."

Maria stopped and sighed. "Cut it out with the spooky pranks. I'm not falling for it."

David reached between branches to shake a tree trunk.

"Are you guys for real? The lights from the drain did something to your grandma?"

A wave of soft clicks, the plastic version of leaves rustling, passed by us. I caught a glimpse of something moving deeper within the trees. It was shorter than me and I thought it ran on four legs.

"Did you hear that?" I hissed.

"Yes." Harold hugged his chest. "Something's in here with us."

"Is it the carolers?" David rubbed his mouth.

"Everyone shut up." Maria pointed upward. "Fake trees don't grow. You're not going to trick me into thinking they do."

We three boys all looked up.

The tops of the fake pines reached into the clouds, as tall as the real pines the neighborhood was named for.

My heart leapt into my throat.

Maria saw the terror on our faces. She looked up. "How did you do that?"

This wasn't a tree farm, it was crushingly dense forest. And despite the incandescent string lights and the impossibly-colored lights from the sewers which now climbed more than ten feet up the trees, shadows still created a thousand hiding places.

"I heard it again!" Harold moaned.

"What?" David whipped around, searching.

I listened as hard as I could.

The carolers' song pierced the air behind us, a stretched out vocalizing of the melody to "The First Noel."

"Run," David ordered, and I was grateful he'd found some confidence.

Plastic scratched at our coats. I stumbled, pressing farther into branches than I meant to, and rubbing against the sewer lights. An assault of Christmas TV specials flooded my brain but my momentum carried me past it.

That sound of plastic clicking came again. Something sprinting through the fake branches just out of sight.

"Why haven't we reached the end yet?" Harold whined.

"Keep running!" David shouted with exaggerated encouragement.

"Something's following us," I warned.

"The carolers?" David asked.

"It doesn't matter," Maria barked through heavy breathes. "Don't slow down. I want out of this weird forest."

The song grew louder. The branches drew closer together. I raised my hands to push them away form my face with my forearms.

"Look!" David yelled.

Ahead, the branches thinned out. I could see the colorful lights of another neighbor's decorations. Relief hit me even as the caroler's song reached a crescendo.

The young woman caroler stepped into our path. She wore a brown wool coat and a bonnet over her hair. Her eyes were pale bluish gray and her nostrils flared in time with the song's rhythm.

The blank patch of skin where her mouth wasn't stretched and constricted like she was chewing on gristle.

Her eyes locked onto mine and she radiated an emotion between hate and intention. There was desire to take me and do... something. I felt the desire but it was entirely foreign. It seeped like thick fog inside me, into the places that had been empty since last Christmas.

The caroler walked toward us.

"This way!" David pushed his way through fake branches.

We followed.

If we could just get around the caroler, we could escape back into the open air.

We stumbled into a little clearing.

We found what had been running between the fake trees. The same thing I'd seen through Harold's window. The same thing I'd seen pressed up against the inside of his TV glass.

Beneath a monolithic plastic Christmas tree stood an animated reindeer.

No, not quite animated. It was painted wood, textured with fabric. Its black eyes tracked me over its not-quite-red nose. Its head was at about my height, but its fabric-lined antlers added another foot. Despite the cloth, those antlers still looked sharp.

The only thing missing was a mouth. The brown fur around his snout had no opening.

"That's Rudolph," Harold whispered.

Just like I'd wanted.

The closer I looked at the reindeer, the more I saw a

weird movement all over his fur, as if his fake skin was slithering over itself.

Next to Rudolph hopped a Jack-in-the-box. Or if I remembered the movie correctly, a "Charlie-in-the-box," a refugee on the Isle of Misfit Toys. Whoever had painted his wooden face had left out his mouth.

His surfaces wriggled like Rudolph's.

Here were the characters I'd been wishing I could watch with Mama and Dad, as if I'd wished them into existence.

The reindeer stomped his hoof. The movement was jerky. His nose shone garishly and emitted an ear-piercing whistle.

The Charlie-in-the-box hopped once, stuttering through the air.

"They're moving in stop motion." David put himself between the models and the rest of us.

"Shut up," whispered Maria.

Rudolph lowered his head, aiming the dagger points of his antlers.

We backed away.

The Charlie-in-the-box sprung forward, flying through the air in a hundred flashes. His accordion belly wrapped around David's leg.

David panicked. He kicked wildly. His leg moved in stuttering glimpses like the reindeer and toy.

He howled in agony.

I wouldn't let my friend suffer the same fate as Harold's grandma.

Apparently, Harold agreed. He'd found his courage.

We both grabbed the box and pulled hard. It wasn't enough.

Maria dug her fingernails underneath the accordion, ripping it away from her little brother.

The toy's clown head whipped back around David's leg and came free. It smacked into my knee.

I felt myself move in stop-motion. It was like getting hit with a two-by-four on every inch of my body, rapid fire.

We flung the Charlie-in-the-box into the trees.

It let out a wheezy accordion noise.

"Look out!" David yelled.

Rudolph was charging. Seven sharpened antlers careened for me and Harold. Harold dove out of the way. I hesitated.

I was already empty. Was "dead" that different?

Maria tackled me. Rudolph passed by.

The young woman caroler caught up to us.

I felt that foreign emotion filling up my empty spaces again. Something like hunger but instead of longing for food itself, it was for the act of cooking an extravagant meal—of creating an extravagant *event*.

The four of us scrambled to our feet and plunged into the trees again.

This time, we spilled out into the neighbor's yard.

8

WE FELL free of the plastic forest.

The carolers' eerie crooning had progressed to the *hallelujahs* of "Angels We Have Heard On High."

David broke the caroler's harmony. "What the hell!"

I turned around to see if the stop-motion demons were still following.

Rudolph and the Charlie-in-the-box slunk behind trees, several rows deep. They weren't advancing.

Maria had stumbled coming out of the trees. She must have hurt herself, because she still knelt in the snow, head down, dark hair hanging over her shoulders.

I expected David to go help, but now that we had a moment to breathe, he was freaking out. "That wasn't real. It couldn't have been real."

I craned my neck back to look up.

The Jones' Christmas tree farm stood sixty feet high,

twice as tall as the houses of Foothill Pines. It hadn't been an illusion inside. The plastic trees had actually grown.

To the side of the forest, those strange string lights crawled up the Jones' house to strangle it. I hoped they'd ran away while we were stuck in the forest.

"I'm serious," David tugged at his hair with both hands. "What the hell is going on? I thought you guys were messing with the Jones."

Harold paced the edge of the yard, watching the stop-motion movie characters slink deeper into the tree farm. "I told you it was real. The lights took my grandma. Oh god. Is she dead? You don't think she's dead, do you?"

I almost told David how we'd seen an eyeball and a pink hair curler and a screaming mouth inside those light-bulbs hanging from Harold's house. But I decided to let the two of them scream their way into David accepting what was happening.

The carolers' song drifted through the fake trees. They weren't getting louder yet. Maybe the one who'd followed us into the tree farm had returned to her companions at the Jones' front door.

From down on her knees in the snow, Maria coughed. Or maybe it was a loud wince.

"Hey." David walked over to his sister. "We've got to figure out what to do. Get up."

Maria tried.

She pushed herself to her feet. Her body rose in rapid-fire stutters. She screamed and her mouth moved like an old film reel.

I'd felt it, too, but only when the Charlie-in-the-Box had been wrapped around me. "Why is she still moving like that?"

"She needs to get farther away from the trees," David said with too much confidence. "She'll be fine. Let's go find Dad."

Maria turned her head toward her little brother. "What's happening?" Her voice skipped like an old record. The mist of her breath came out in quick, stuttering spurts. Maria brought her hand to her mouth because of the pain but doubled over.

"Yeah, we need Dad." David's voice cracked.

"The puppet things stayed in the forest," Harold whined. "Why is this still happening?"

David cleared his throat. "Guys, help me carry Maria."

He and Harold picked up her legs and I put my hands on her back to keep her from falling backward.

But as they lifted and I kept her balanced, we all four moved with that stop-motion stuttering. Again, it was like getting hit with a two-by-four over every inch of my body.

I collapsed, letting Maria tumble backwards.

Harold fell over, grabbing his stomach. David gritted his teeth and tried to catch Maria on his own. They both hit the grass.

Maria sat up. I saw a rip in her jeans marred with blood.

When she'd pushed me out of the way, Rudolph's antler had cut her.

I worried that what had been squirming on Rudolph's outside had made it into Maria's insides.

She climbed to her feet, jerking in pain. "Go get Dad."

I almost sprinted for home to get Dad, but of course she was telling David to get Mr. Perez.

"We can't leave you here," David said.

Maria didn't respond. I couldn't blame her. It *hurt* to move in stop-motion.

"Douglas." David held back tears, but he was getting his feet under him, shifting into problem-solving mode. "Give her your coat. Yours will fit."

I didn't argue that she already had a sweater on and I'd be cold without it.

"We'll get Dad and come right back," David promised.

But before we ran up the road, David pulled his Leatherman multitool from his pocket. He cut a length of not-red and not-purple Christmas lights from the fake trees and stuffed it in his pocket. "Okay, let's go."

We ran up the road.

9

As we ran up the hill toward David's cul-de-sac, Harold slowed down in front of a yard filled with inflatable decorations and buzzing with their motors.

"We have to warn the Bakers," Harold said.

They had a girl in the grade above us, Tiffany. Harold liked her. He crushed on every girl with a pretty face.

David turned around to answer Harold, but he kept jogging backward up the road. "I'm worried about Maria right now."

Behind us, the carolers came around the plastic tree farm that reached so high into the sky.

Lights crawled beneath the snow on either side of the street, wires creeping through yards, bulbs flickering to life just beneath the surface to create a not-red or not-purple patch of snow. The lights' progress kept pace with the carolers' advance.

I watched to make sure that they didn't notice Maria, frozen at the edge of the fake trees.

"We have to warn Tiffany," Harold insisted.

"Then you two knock on more doors. I'm sure they'll believe you just like the Jones did. I'm going to get my dad."

David jogged on ahead.

Harold took a worried glance back at the approaching carolers. I'd rather have stayed with David, but he told me to go with Harold.

I wanted so badly to go with David instead of Harold that I almost started existing again. But I was still empty. And with my last-ditch Christmas Eve plan falling apart, what was I even doing now? All year I'd been anxiously awaiting Christmas so Mama and Dad could be happy again. Then when they ignored the start of the season and I made my plan, I spent all of December excited to show them my light display. And now it'd been swallowed and perverted by the lights from the drain.

If we made it through tonight, then what? Back to a quiet home of Dad watching old sitcoms on VHS, and Mama sitting in her chair with unmoving knitting needles in her lap.

If I got stop-motioned into pieces or if I got dissected like Harold's grandma, would there be any mass inside my empty shell to fill a single lightbulb?

"Come on," Harold ordered and I followed.

We jogged up the front walk of the Bakers' house. Their driveway was filled with the cars of visiting family and their yard was filled with inflatables. Mickey Mouse with a Santa hat, the Grinch with a Santa hat, Winnie the Pooh with a Santa hat, Santa Claus with his white hair uncovered.

I looked up at the grinning Grinch. Its smooth surface was pressed outward by unsteady air pressure. The way the flat canvas portrayed his red felt clothes and green furry body was uncanny. The fake white fluff ball on the top of the Grinch's hat seemed higher than it had been earlier today. "Were these always so big?" I asked.

But Harold was on a mission. He was already on Tiffany's front porch, banging on the door. I caught up to him.

Muffled Christmas music played "Jingle Bell Rock," which was a nice interruption to the eerie vocalizing of the carolers.

I checked on their progress. They'd passed Maria. The random pattern of lights beneath the snow had grown without touching her.

I relaxed a little, now that she was safe. The carolers were almost to the edge of Tiffany's yard. We'd have to run to the next house through the snow.

Harold banged on the door again. "I hear them in there, don't you?"

I put my ear to the door. Beneath the classic electric guitar of the song was an underwater warbling. And within that, I did hear people. "I hear crying. Or laughing?"

It was a muffled cacophony of sobbing and cheering

and moaning and laughing, all mixed with a shrill, reverberating echo.

"We have to help." Harold turned the knob freely and pushed inward. The door gave only a little. It cracked enough to let out the still-muffled song.

"Something's blocking it," Harold said. "Help me push."

We both shoved on the door, straining against something that gave and held firm in a way that reminded me of a waterbed.

"On three," Harold said.

He counted and then we pushed together.

Resistance gave and the door swung open. As soon as it was open wide, a stiff curtain charged at us.

My heart jumped to my throat. I leapt away, fearing I was about to be devoured by this thing advancing at impossible speeds.

But it hit the open doorway and stopped. White canvas pressed out against the empty rectangle, a patch of a balloon too large to fit through.

Not a balloon. An inflatable yard decoration.

"What the hell is this?" Harold smacked it.

A muffled, garbled voice came from inside. "Is someone out there? I can't get my eyes open."

"Hello?" Harold smacked the canvas again. "We're out here. We can help."

"No!" they screamed. "It's too much."

We heard a sound like someone getting beaten with those inflatable boxing gloves. Then more pained howls came through.

"Do you have a pocket knife?" Harold asked me.

I shook my head.

He searched the front porch for anything sharp, but came up empty.

He tried to grab the surface with his fingertips and rip. It didn't work.

The howling inside turned to sobs, then laughter, then sharp screams.

I knew what I wanted now. I wanted to get home. But Harold was still trying to help so that's what I did, too.

"Should we try around back?" I suggested.

We both checked on the carolers' progress. They were at the end of Tiffany's front walk.

"I don't want to get left too far in their wake." Harold stuck his gloved hands in his armpits. He rocked on his heels. "What do we do?"

I didn't have an answer. I was watching the carolers, who hadn't moved on from the front walk that led right to the Bakers' porch where we were standing.

Patterns of not-red and not-purple filled the downhill side of Tiffany's front yard, waiting.

"They're gloating," Harold said. "They love what they've done to Tiffany."

Maybe. But they weren't looking at the house. They were looking at me.

"Let's catch up with David," Harold said. "He'll figure out what to do."

We ran from the Bakers' home, leaving them to whatever was happening behind those inflatable walls.

10

We ran through snowy yards, parallel to the carolers' path up the street. Wind pierced my hoodie, making me regret leaving my coat with Maria. Snow dampened my pant legs above my boots.

We needed to get to David's house quick. If the carolers and their vining light strands didn't kill me, the cold might.

Past the Bakers' house lived an old woman I didn't know. She had blow molds of Mary and Joseph and manger for Baby Jesus. Each day during December, she'd moved three blow molds of the Wise Men on camels a little closer to the manger. Tonight on Christmas Eve, they'd finally made it.

Lights flickered to life beneath the snow, painting a path from the Bakers' inflatables to the glowing Holy Family.

We didn't stick around to see what they did to Jesus.

With the carolers' slow pace, we easily gained ground.

They wordlessly sang "Bring a Torch, Jeanette, Isabella," which I'd caught Mama humming last week, before she noticed what she was doing and slipped away to her bedroom to cry.

The next house was on the corner of Pine Whisper Way and David's cul-de-sac. Foothill Pines ended another hundred feet up the hill, and then the foothills turned to mountains.

A working toy train, as tall as my bicycle, ran on tracks in the corner house's yard. It pulled miniature cabin cars. For the past week, the man there had give rides to the littler neighborhood kids. Erica rode that train last year, the night before she died. Maybe'd she snuck out because she wanted another ride.

Tonight, the train sat still.

Harold and I cut over the tracks to sprint into David's cul-de-sac and past the six houses on either side. David's house was at the very end.

We came up to Mr. Perez yelling at David on their front porch, while hastily putting on his boots. "You left her there?"

"I came to get you," David sobbed.

Mr. Perez saw me and Harold. "You two didn't stay with her, either? Douglas, where's your coat? Do your parents know you're outside? After what happened last year? *Hijole.*"

He'd been the one to find Erica, tripping over her frozen body.

"All three of you, get inside. You two, call your parents. Douglas, you first. I'll go get Maria."

"You can't move her," Harold said. "It hurts."

Mr. Perez furled his brow at us panicking kids. "Go inside." He tromped up the road, toward the singing.

To his left, above the houses, lights from Pine Whisper Way glowed brighter and brighter.

David might still believe that his dad could solve anything, but I'd learned firsthand of problems that grownups couldn't fix.

"Is he gonna be okay?" Harold asked.

David breathed deep. He was trying not to cry. "My dad runs marathons and builds houses. He'll get Maria home just fine."

I wasn't sure he believed that. Regardless, David had a role he wanted to play. "When he gets back, we'll have a plan ready for how to stop the carolers and the lights."

"And bring my grandma back," Harold added.

I'd seen Mrs. Bancroft's eyeball inside of a bulbous Christmas light. I didn't have much hope for bringing her back.

"Yeah," David cautiously agreed. "It's Christmas Eve. Miracles, right?"

He twitched a little like people did when they remembered Erica and thought they'd put their foot in their mouth. I didn't call him out.

"Right," Harold hugged his chest. "She'll be okay."

David gave me a concerned look. "First we need a plan." He pulled from his pocket the length of invasive Christmas light wire that he'd cut from the Jones' tree farm. The bulbs still glowed dimly.

"Let's go," he said.

"Where?" I asked.

"My workshop."

A couple years back, we'd played in the shed behind his house nearly every day, solving fake mysteries with the science kit he'd received from a Christmas charity.

I didn't want to go to his workshop. I didn't want to be Encyclopedia Brown or a Hardy Boy. I just wanted this night to be over.

But I followed David and Harold around the side of the house.

11

Around David's house, the back yard was its own gentle slope down to the wooded gulch. The old shed—David's "workshop"—was the only thing rising above the untouched snow.

"Should we tell your mom?" Harold asked.

"Not yet." David stomped a path through the snow. "She probably thinks Dad's still giving it to me out front. We have a few minutes."

We all shuffled into the dark shed. David shut the door behind us.

It was a shelter from the wind. I didn't feel warm, but at least the cold wasn't gusting under my hoodie anymore.

In the total darkness, I could almost disappear. It felt nice.

A chain clicked and a dangling lightbulb switched on.

Yard tools occupied most of the scant space. David

dragged a grimy lawnmower off to the side so he could access the workbench against the back wall.

Atop the workbench sat a cracked old briefcase.

David blew off the dust and opened the case.

Inside were magnifying glasses, tweezers, syringes, and lying on its side, a microscope.

David set it on the workbench, right side up. Its weight *thunked* on the plywood. He wiped the lens with his shirt. He handed me a flashlight. "The microscope light quit working. Point that right at the bottom."

He placed the light strand under the microscope. I aimed the flashlight right at it.

David peered into the lens. He twisted a dial on the side.

"What do you see?" Harold asked.

"We should have brought some regular wire as a control. But even still, this isn't normal. Look." He stepped away and motioned for me to look through the lens.

I obliged.

It took a moment for me to understand what I was looking at. The dark green of the wire filled the entire view.

Magnified a hundred times, the wires seemed to be woven from a thousand tiny threads, and each of those from ten thousand fraying hairs. The minuscule hairs wiggled under the light.

"What's that remind you of?" David asked.

I wasn't in the mood for dumbass questions. I wondered where I could sit and hide until it was safe to go home or until my emptiness spread and I stopped existing entirely.

"Let me see," Harold said. He forced the flashlight into my hand.

I held it steady for him without complaint.

"Looks like a poison ivy vine," Harold said.

"But it's moving," David said.

Harold looked back into the microscope. "Is it?"

David pushed him aside to get another look. "They stopped. It must not live that long after I cut it off."

"Like a real vine," Harold said.

"Which means it has roots," I said as the thought came to my mind. "Down in the storm drain."

I immediately regretted speaking.

"I'm not going down there," Harold said.

"Of course not," David said.

I noticed something strange happening on the workbench. "Guys." I aimed the flashlight next to the microscope. Glass slides were strewn about.

Three of them had grown in size and twisted, sprouting appendages to become festive glass snowflakes that my grandma might hang from her tree.

David gasped excitedly. Harold groaned and backed away.

David picked one up and put it under the microscope. He peered down through the lens. "The strange pieces are made of those same hairs. The wire reached over and changed things before it died."

I pointed to the workbench. "Why'd it skip that one?"

Three slides were mutated, but the thin strands had snaked around one slide, avoiding it in a big loop, to then latch onto another.

Harold, now curious, leaned over the bench. "The slide it skipped has already got something in it."

David picked it up. "Yeah, this came with the set. It's a dried spider egg."

He spoke more quickly as he reached a conclusion. "The hairs only went for the empty slides."

"The lights from the sewer started with the empty houses," I said. I used to love solving mysteries with David.

"They want an empty place to grow?" Harold asked.

"That's my guess," David said. "And it's camouflage. It looks like what's around it. We've got the Christmas lights contest, so that's how it's trying to blend in."

"It's doing a shit job," Harold said.

"We're the only one's who've paid attention before it was too late," David said. "I'd say it's working, dumbass." Now that he was puzzling through a mystery, David was more naturally taking charge.

"Why'd it go to my house if it wasn't empty?" Harold asked. "Or the Jones? Or Tiffany's house?"

David stepped away from the microscope. "What happened at Tiffany's house?"

Harold told him about the inflatable canvas pressing outward from their doorway. I added the part about their echoing screams inside.

"Wow." David exhaled. "We might not have much time

to solve this if we want to save everybody. Probably just tonight."

I had no idea where he'd come up with that.

"Why'd it go after everyone else if their houses weren't empty?" Harold asked again.

"It's not just houses that can be empty," I said, but they ignored me.

"Your parents are out of town," David said. "Maybe that counts as empty? But the Jones and the Bakers, why would it go after them?"

I imagined myself on both their porches, and I knew what they had in common.

"It probably starts with the empty ones," Harold said, "and then moves on to whatever's closest."

That didn't feel true. There was another connection between the empty houses and Harold's house, but I wasn't ready to say it out loud, yet.

"What happens next?" Harold asked. "We know it wants empty places. What do we do now?"

"My Dad has plenty of weed killer in here. He hates dandelions. Let's try it on the Christmas lights. If it works, we spray all the lights we can find. When we kill enough of them, the whole plant should die."

"No." The word came out of my mouth before I could stop it. But I let it hang there.

"What?" David demanded.

"Nevermind."

"What's wrong with my plan?"

We had a terrible poison ivy problem in our yard.

Spraying the vines killed those vines, but then the roots kept growing, putting out new vines. My dad taught me that. "Nothing's wrong," I said.

"Oh my god," Harold complained. "Say it."

I didn't want to push my own ideas but it was harder to say no to Harold.

"We have to spray the roots," I said softly. "I pulled the lights from a storm drain. The roots are in the sewer."

"I'm not going down there," Harold declared.

"We don't have to," David said. Then without any proof except his own assertion, he said, "we don't have to spray the roots. Plants need their leaves to live. We kill enough of the lights and the whole thing will die. Okay?"

I didn't say anything.

"Douglas." David leaned toward me. "Okay?"

Of course I was right. But I said, "Okay."

"We'll spray the lights," David repeated. "Let's take this around front for when my dad gets back with Maria."

"What about the carolers?" Harold asked.

David chewed on his lip. "They must be connected."

"No shit," Harold said. "They sing and the lights grow."

"I mean literally connected by the little hairs."

"Let's spray them with weedkiller," I said. They weren't the roots, but something about spraying those mouthless horrors felt like I would enjoy it.

"We'll start with just a light strand. That seems safer than getting the carolers mad."

"Grandma," Harold said. "I want to spray the lights on the lightbulb with my grandma's lips."

David and I looked at each other. If David recognized the problem, I wasn't going to speak up.

"We'll try the wires first. Then the carolers. See what happens. Maybe we can find something else they transformed and spray that to make sure it changes back, instead of... you know. Just dying."

Harold rocked on his heels anxiously, but he nodded.

David dug around behind the lawnmower until he brought out a plastic jug with a black hand pump on top, and a hose with a spray wand coming out the side.

"Help me fill this up," he said.

I helped balance the RoundUp jug while he poured it into the sprayer.

"Whichever of you is humming," David said, "cut it out."

A muffled vocalizing was making its way into the shed.

Harold let out a noise between a sigh and moan. "The carolers."

"Why are they coming this way?" I asked, already knowing the answer. "They skipped the other cul-de-sacs. Why are they coming down yours?"

David doubled down on his mystery-solver mode. "I must have more neighbors out of town than the other side streets. More empty houses. This thing wants to camouflage itself in emptiness."

I hugged my arms across my chest, wanting to fill myself with warmth. This shed was chilly.

David pumped the sprayer until each downward thrust required his entire bodyweight. He turned the handle to lock it into place. "Harold, you're the strongest, you carry it. I'm the best shot with a Super Soaker, so I'll aim the wand. Douglas, you help Harold if he gets tired. Everybody ready?"

The shed door swung open.

The carolers' song grew clearer.

Harold screamed.

David aimed the spray wand at the open door before his mom began shouting.

"What are you boys doing out here?" She switched into Spanish, screaming at David, then back into English for me. "Do your parents know you're out here? They must be scared to death. And after last year?"

Mrs. Perez' lip quivered. At Erica's funeral, she'd cried louder than anyone. Dad thought she was putting on a show until Mama convinced him that Mrs. Perez was a sensitive woman who wore her heart on her sleeve.

Mama and Dad.

Oh god.

How long had it been since I'd left the house?

I'd set the alarm on my TV to switch on full volume only half an hour from when I'd left.

"Mama! Dad!" I pushed past Mrs. Perez to run out into the snow.

12

I MADE it to David's front yard before Mrs. Perez caught me and grabbed my shoulders to yank me to a stop. I felt her loosen as she looked up.

The four carolers walked down the short street, directly toward us. In their wake, winter was alight with uncanny colors.

The storm drains in the curb glowed not-purple and not-red. String lights grew across the road and covered houses like invasive kudzu.

Houses had grown new decorations, turning the straight lines and right angles of suburbia into jagged lines of bulbs and jutting portrayals of Santa and his reindeer.

Two doors down, Mrs. Driscoll stood in the snow wearing red Christmas pajamas, screaming and crying over a blow mold candy cane.

Across the street, Mr. Green hurried down his porch to go help his neighbor. He tripped over a decorative "To

Santa" mailbox. I didn't see him get back up, but the pile of letters on the ground grew tall enough to smother the mailbox.

The carolers were close enough for me to see their faces. Above the empty patches of skin where their mouths should be, their eyes watched me eagerly.

From this distance, I felt a touch of that hungry expectation.

I didn't care what they wanted from me. I had to find my parents.

I couldn't see around the corner down Pine Whisper Way. Had Mama and Dad come looking for me already? Had they been caught?

Mrs. Perez slowly pulled me toward their porch, away from the approaching carolers. "Do you know who they are?"

I heard fear in her whisper. She realized they weren't natural as quickly as I had.

"They were in the sewer," I said.

"What's wrong with their faces?"

David and Harold caught up with us.

"It's all plants," David said. "I've got Dad's weedkiller."

Mrs. Perez heard the determination in her sons voice, which must have scared her. "Where is your father?"

"He went down the street to help Maria."

Mrs. Perez reared up like a snake ready to strike. "And why did Maria need help?"

David stumbled over the answer, so I said, "She got

stuck. I thought they'd be back by now. We should go find them."

A gust of wind picked up the pile of letters to Santa.

Mrs. Perez jumped. "David, take your friends inside. I'll go get your father."

Harold started to obey. I wasn't going inside until I found Mama and Dad.

David dug in his heels. "I'm coming, too. We have to try the RoundUp on the lights."

Police sirens joined the caroling and then grew louder.

"Someone called 911!" Harold said with relief.

Flashing red and blue reached the intersection before the cruiser did. The siren wailed, drowning out the carols.

But when it came into view, it wasn't a police cruiser anymore. A sedan-sized lawn decoration of Santa's sleigh slid up the hill, dragging a web of not-red and not-purple Christmas lights behind it. The siren noise curved into a quiet chorus of jingling bells. The cruiser lost its momentum and skidded to a stop.

Blue and red tinsel decorated the sides, with a white stripe across the middle. The same colors as our town's police cars. Inside the sleigh sat a plastic Santa in a blue felt suit with white fringe. It wore a pistol at its side.

"No," whined Harold.

"Inside," Mrs. Perez ordered.

David instead ran up the sidewalk, lugging the garden sprayer at his side.

I followed him, needing to find my parents who I'd unwittingly lured into this festive nightmare.

13

DAVID LUGGED the two-gallon sprayer over onto the sidewalk to avoid the carolers.

I followed.

I didn't think David's plan of spraying as many light strands as possible was going to work. But it might carve enough of a path for me to look for Mama and Dad.

Harold followed a moment later. "We have to try spraying my grandma."

The carolers still sang their wordless song, now the vocalized melody of "I Saw Three Ships Come Sailing In."

David's neighbor Mrs. Driscoll still sobbed over the candy cane blow mold. She was trying to pick it up but kept hesitating to touch it. "Help me!" she cried.

Mrs. Perez chased after us. She slowed down to consider helping her neighbor, but protecting her son was the higher priority.

She pushed me aside to grab David around his chest. "I told you to go back inside."

"We have to help!" David protested.

Harold gasped. "Mrs. Perez, look out!"

The carolers had turned their attention to us, no longer walking straight down the street.

All four of them stared at me with that hungry look that the young woman had given me in the Jones' tree farm. They had plans for me.

David tossed the sprayer to Harold. With the weight of the herbicide, it was a weak throw, but Harold managed to catch it before it hit the icy concrete.

Mrs. Perez carried David back down the sidewalk. "You boys come with me."

"Spray the lights!" David said.

Harold held the sprayer like a football and ran toward Pine Whisper Way. He didn't care about the lights. He only wanted to turn his grandma back.

"Harold, you dumbass!" David shouted.

Regardless of Harold's goals, if the weedkiller could cut a path through the invasive Christmas decorations and downhill, then that was how I'd find Mama and Dad. I ran after Harold, nearly tripping over a mailbox that had mutated into a brick chimney. I caught myself on the bricks, feeling thousands of tiny vines squirm beneath my fingers. In the darkness inside the chimney, something moved.

"Douglas!" Mrs. Perez barked my name. "Think of your parents."

In her mind, that meant to get inside and keep myself safe. But Mama and Dad were probably out here looking for me.

I pushed myself off the bricks and ran after Harold. Every step of the way I had to dance between glowing patches beneath the snow, and sidestep mutated mailboxes or landscaping.

I felt the carolers' gaze follow me.

Behind me, Mrs. Perez grunted. David's shoes slapped on the icy pavement. He yelled to his mom, "I have to do this. Go help Mrs. Driscoll."

I turned around to see David running to catch up with me and Harold. His Mom followed, but the carolers had changed their direction to follow me.

Mrs. Perez crashed into the old bearded caroler.

A shudder passed through the carolers. The impact separated the millions of vertical vines that made up their clothes and their flesh.

After another moment, they righted themselves and continued walking.

Mrs. Perez backed away into the mailbox that had been transformed into a brick chimney. She leaned against it. "What are you people?"

The carolers didn't answer.

I stopped to yell, "Don't touch that!"

A green furry hand with long fingertips shot up out from the chimney. Covering its wrist was the white fluff of the sleeve of a Santa Claus coat. The hand snapped down to feel its way along the bricks.

"Look out!" I started running back toward Mrs. Perez, which only served as a distraction to her.

The green hairy fingers found her shoulder. They patted once, twice, three times, to make sure that it understood what it was feeling. Then it took hold of her shoulder between its thumb and forefinger.

"Mom!" David had turned around by this point. "Harold, bring the sprayer back!"

Mrs. Perez swatted at the green hand. It lifted her by the shoulder off the ground, higher until the red-velvet sleeve extended ten feet above the chimney and Mrs. Perez dangled, kicking and fighting.

I ran for her but the carolers' slow walk brought them into my path.

David abandoned his wait for the sprayer. He sprinted around the carolers, just in time to watch that green furry hand jerk his mom down the chimney.

14

DAVID'S SCREAM reminded me of Mama's.

He stood on his toes to reach the top of the chimney, reaching his arm as deep inside as he could.

I caught up. It was a black square at the top of the bricks, hardly big enough to fit David's arm. There was no way Mrs. Perez should have fit down there.

Just like there was no way that a string of Christmas lights could have mutated a mailbox into a chimney in the first place.

David's coat sleeve ripped on the rough edge of the bricks. He kept trying to climb inside.

We didn't have time for David to regain control of himself. The carolers were on top of us. I grabbed his arm and pulled.

He let me guide him around the carolers and toward Harold, who stood frozen at the intersection of David's cul-de-sac and Pine Whisper Way.

I looked down the hill.

Where the road around us was dangerously filled with not-red and not-purple glows beneath the snow, down the hill, those lights had risen above the street. They hung between houses, as thick as an impassable jungle.

"I couldn't have gotten there in time," Harold said.

"You ran off!" David shook free of my grasp. He punched Harold in the mouth.

Harold shrugged it off. "You told me to take the sprayer and go."

"Not this far! Just far enough to spray without my mom stopping you." His voice cracked. "Oh god, Mom! What am I gonna tell my dad?"

This time, it was Harold who gave me a knowing look. Wasn't David being unreasonably hopeful? Despite the fact that Harold himself was hoping that RoundUp would put his grandma back together again. They were both expecting Christmas miracles.

I didn't remember going through a denial phase with Erica.

"Where do we go?" Harold asked me.

David paced in the snow, yelling at himself in a mix of Spanish and English.

I wanted to go home. But the road down the hill was covered in Christmas lights and strange decorations.

David was panicking. Harold didn't know the neighborhood as well as I did. As empty as I knew I was, in that moment I had no choice but to exist. "Spraying the leaves won't kill it. We have to get the roots. We need to get down into the gulch and into the sewer."

We both looked back at the carolers. Their slow pace would give us time.

But my denial of David's plan snapped him out of his panic. "That's too dangerous. If we want to bring everyone back, we have to stay alive ourselves. Plants need leaves to survive. We spray enough up here and the whole thing will die."

I slipped back inside myself.

Harold said, "David, I think-"

"Spray the lights!" David yelled.

Harold started downhill.

A strand of lights hung loose from one rooftop to another, drooping all the way down to touch the snowy pavement. Harold soaked it in weed killer.

The not-red and not-purple lights went dim. Flakes fell from the wire itself until it lost enough structure to break in two and fall to the icy street.

David perked up. "I knew it," he whispered. "Keep going!"

Harold sprayed deeper into the web of lights that criss-crossed the street.

I glanced behind us. Even with their slow steps, the carolers gained on us.

"Let me do it," David ordered Harold. "You do the pump."

Harold set the jug on the ground to pump the handle. David aimed the sprayer. He killed another three lights strands, a blow mold of a lumpy peppermint candy, and a wrapped present tied with hundreds of sloppy ribbons.

Harold kicked apart the box as it turned gray. Pieces blew away in the wind. He hefted the jug and we advanced another five feet.

They did it all again, pumping, spraying, kicking apart any dead lights that remained in our way.

I stayed at their side.

The decay wasn't spreading. Whatever David sprayed died, but that death didn't spread to the rest of the vines.

David's plan wasn't working. In fact, as we carved our way downhill, what we'd really done was burrow our way into a dead-end.

The jug was half-empty. We'd only managed to carve a path fifteen feet long and just wide enough for us to pass through.

The carolers were about to reach our starting point and cut us off.

"David," I said. "It's not working."

"Of course it is. The vines are dying. They're plants and we're killing them."

I needed to argue with him. The carolers were getting closer. But there was no convincing David of anything. At least, I couldn't do it.

Harold, however, saw my concern. "David. We're trapping ourselves in here."

"Guys, it's working. We can't give up now." He was manic from watching his mom disappear. "We have to get to my dad. He'll know how to help mom."

He wasn't trying to kill the lights. He was making a path to where we'd left Maria, where he hoped to find his dad. But even though I could see the fake trees rising forty feet above the rest of this madness, we were still two houses away. We'd either run out of weed killer or the carolers would catch up to us.

"David," I said as strongly as I could. My anger didn't phase him. "We don't know where your dad is."

"He's with Maria. And we're killing it. Watch." David sprayed a spiral of icicle lights that had been suspended by nothing. They dissolved into plasticky ash.

I looked to Harold for help. He took over. "You said it would spread. Once we killed the leaves, the plant would die. How many leaves do we have to kill? This thing isn't dying."

"It'll work!" David yelled.

"Maybe Douglas was right. We have to kill the roots."

David stopped answering. The sprayer lost pressure.

Harold stood over the pumping handle, unmoving. "We need a different plan."

Movement behind us.

We all three turned around.

Fifteen feet uphill, at the entrance of our carved path through the invasive Christmas decorations, the carolers blocked our retreat.

15

"WHY ARE they even coming over here?" Harold said. "I thought they were going after empty places."

I'm empty, I thought.

"Oh, I was stupid," David said. "We made an empty spot in their tangle of lights. Now they want to fill it again."

I told you, I didn't say.

"We have to spray a path out," David said. "To Maria and then behind the Jones' house."

"We can't make it that far," Harold argued. "We have to cut over right now."

"That's my sister! You can't tell me to leave her. You don't have a sister—you don't know what it would feel like!"

Harold didn't know, but I did. I touched David's elbow. "We can't reach her before the carolers get to us. We have to cut over right now."

David glared at me. "Fine. See if you can slow them down."

It sounded dumb, considering how slow they already walked.

As David sprayed toward the Bakers' house, Harold scooped up chunks of ice. He hurled one into the old man caroler's chest. It stuck there. The million tiny vines that made up his body squirmed, their colors and textures overlapping and getting out of place. They pushed the piece of ice out. It fell on the street and shattered.

The effort to expel the ice did slow the carolers' advance, ever so slightly.

But it wasn't enough. If we made it out of this tangle of Christmas lights and behind the houses, then what? If I wanted to keep helping, I wouldn't be able to convince David that his plan was no good. If I left him and Harold to go find Mama and Dad, then what? Hide at home with them until more police came?

That's not what I wanted.

I didn't want any of this. I wanted Christmas. I'd looked forward to it all year. I'd imagined a thousand ways that Mama and Dad would be happy again once Christmas came.

Now that wasn't going to happen. Even if they were still alive, this was a second life-shattering Christmas.

I wanted to disappear. To slip away back home and return to my daydreams from this morning, of my parents seeing my little light display and realizing that I'm not empty. That I still love Christmas.

But I was surrounded by kudzu Christmas lights and chased by mouthless carolers.

And I still couldn't bring myself to push back against David.

I couldn't run away because there was nowhere and no one to run to.

I couldn't be empty anymore. I had to exist. I had an idea for stopping them and I had to fight for it.

"They came from the sewer," I said. "My dad says weedkiller only works if you get the roots. The Christmas lights' roots are in the sewer."

"I don't want to go down there," Harold said. "But we might need to."

David said, "We're the only ones who know what's going on. We can't put ourselves in that sort of risk."

I gathered everything I had to shout at my friend. I discovered it wasn't much. "We have to kill the roots!"

I felt even more empty than I had before.

"He's probably right," Harold said.

I knew I was right. I suspected David didn't agree because he hadn't come up with it and he was determined to be the hero.

If I could make one more argument for my plan, David might go along with it. But voicing my opinion was all the existence I could muster. I couldn't insist on it.

The carolers walked closer, down this holiday gauntlet we'd carved.

"What do we do?" Harold asked David.

David sprayed a spiderweb of lights and we broke free behind the Bakers' house. "Fine. We'll go into the sewer."

16

DAVID LED the way down beside the Bakers' house.

The whole house bulged outward. Vinyl siding cracked and the brick foundation had visibly rounded.

On the other side of the windows, something massive pressed the curtains flat against the glass. The reverberating screams and laughter had died, or at least grown quieter than the wind and the vocalized carols.

The snow behind the Bakers' and Jones' house was spotted with lights. We high-stepped around them, over the hidden wires beneath the snow.

David avoided looking at me, no doubt still mad that we weren't soaking the lights in weedkiller right now.

"The carolers aren't still following us, are they?" Harold asked.

"They shouldn't be," David said. "There's plenty of empty houses back that way."

"But they followed us where we killed the wires."

"Because we made an empty space. They're not following us anymore. We're fine."

I didn't say what I'd already realized. Why they'd gone from Harold's house, to David's, to our carved path through the infested street.

I'd pointed my friends to the way they could fix the problem. That was all I could bring myself to do.

We passed the Bakers' toolshed, its door hanging open. Gardening tools hung inside.

Harold pointed to a pair of gardening shears. "Grab those. There'll be some poetic justice in using Tiffany's giant scissors to cut up some of these lights."

"We're not writing a poem," David said.

But I took the shears anyways. The cold of their wood handles seeped through my gloves. They had a comfortable weight to them.

At the bottom of the back yard, strands of not-purple and not-red lights hung in the tree line.

They didn't reach any deeper into the forest, down into the gulch. It was like they were creating a wall to keep us in.

"Over there." Harold pointed to an opening where a light strand was caught on a low branch. It created a gate we could duck under.

We slipped beneath the dangling loop of Christmas lights and into the forest.

The woods created an instant buffer against the droning carols. Snow gathered on branches where they met tree trunks. It sprinkled the tops of bushes.

The gulch was a buffer against the wind, as well. My hoodie kept me a little warmer down here.

I could run home.

It wasn't my job to save the neighborhood. I couldn't.

But Mama and Dad wouldn't be home. They'd be out looking for me. Maybe already grabbed by the lights.

I followed David down the steep hill, deeper into the gulch, where we'd played countless afternoons. The creek at the bottom was dry, only running in the spring and summer when snowmelt poured down from the mountains.

I slipped on a rock but caught myself on a young, bendy pine tree.

"How will we know what the roots look like?" Harold asked. "Won't it be Christmas camouflage like the vines? Or will it look like cement pipes down in the sewer?"

We reached the snowy creek bed.

David continued upstream toward the sewer drain. "Ask Douglas. This is his plan."

I wanted to snap at him. We'd tried his idea and it didn't work. But if I argued, then he'd have a response, and what was the point?

"There's no one down there," I guessed. "It won't need camouflage."

"Is it that smart?" Harold asked. "Isn't it a plant?"

I didn't know. It knew where it wanted to go. It had chased me with characters from the movie I'd been wanting to watch. "Seems like it thinks," I said.

We continued through the pines.

The four-foot cement pipe came into view.

The light of David's flashlight revealed dark stains on the floor of the pipe where each spring, snowmelt rubbed dirt and trash against the cement.

"Turn off the light for a second," I whispered.

Harold obliged.

Without that incandescent yellow glow, a different light became visible, deep within the tunnel.

I hefted the shears, appreciating their weight.

Weedkiller sloshed in the jug that Harold carried. "Ready?" he asked.

"As we'll ever be," David complained, but he led the way inside.

17

WITHOUT ANY SNOWMELT, the cement tunnel was bone dry.

I learned in my Earth Science class that most caves in our region stayed at sixty-two degrees. And although a frigid draft blew past us, it was still warmer than outside.

The deeper we walked, the warmer it got.

I decided it made sense for Maria to have my coat now. If she was still alive up there.

David's flashlight provided plenty of light in the claustrophobic space, although with me and Harold behind him, his own body created a shadow where we needed to step. I kicked through rocks and sticks.

As we approached the first catch basin, a not-red and not-purple glow grew strong enough for us to see it despite the flashlight.

We crawled out from the pipe and into a cement box. This was one of the many intersections beneath Foothill Pines. There were three more openings: one to a pipe uphill, one downhill, and one leading at an upward slope, toward the street.

A string of lights slithered across the cement floor, emerging from the pipe on our left and exiting to our right, uphill.

I tested out the shears. They snapped real nice.

"Do it," Harold said.

I hooked one blade under the wires. As the wire continued its journey, each bulb clicked against the metal.

I jerked the handles apart. The blades snapped together, snipping the light strand in two.

David let out a little grunt of triumph.

The uphill end of the wire stopped its forward trajectory. Its bulbs dimmed and it writhed around like a snake in its death throes.

The end of the downhill side flailed about just as much. Granular white powder poured from its broken end: fake snow.

"That's the stuff that covered up my grandma," Harold said. "Don't let it touch you."

The flailing end of the wire calmed down and then continued its slithering path uphill, wrapping around the dying vine I'd cut through. The dimming bulbs regained their brightness.

"We have to kill the roots," I whispered.

David pointed the light down the pipe where the light strands were coming from. In the quiet, we heard the wire and bulbs scraping on the cement, dragging leaves and sticks. "How do we get down there without touching the wires?" he asked with too much smugness.

I took the lead. I leaned against one side of the pipe with my hands, positioning my feet on the opposite side to avoid the wires at the bottom. "There's space to walk next to them."

"Maybe for you," David shot back.

Harold followed behind me, straddling the wires and hunched forward.

"You guys are insane." David came last, his light flashing ahead with me and Harold blocking it.

I considered reaching down to cut the wires again. Either the weapon in my hands, or the experience of lightly harming the weird lights, gave me a strange feeling. Not the hope and excitement I'd felt when planning my decoration reveal to my parents. But similar to what I'd anticipated feeling afterwards.

It wasn't enough, though. I still wanted... what? To save the neighborhood? To kill this thing so I could look for Mama and Dad?

Yes, but there was something else. Something related to the same reason I'd decorated that empty house in the first place. I couldn't quite wrap my mind around it yet.

I carefully stepped past the still-moving wires.

Deeper into the hillside, we reached the catch basin where I'd first seen the lights and carolers.

"It's not far now," I said. This felt good. Saying my thoughts out loud. Letting myself exist beyond the confines of myself.

"How do you know?" Harold asked.

"This is where I first saw them." I pointed to the rectangular gap in the top corner of the cement box.

The string of lights that I'd hooked and pulled out earlier still crawled up out of the drain and into Foothill Pines.

I opened the shears and cut the light strand.

But like before, even though the bulbs went dim for a moment, the surviving strand wrapped itself around the dying half, and everything kept growing.

"That won't work," David said.

I looked up out of the drain, standing where the carolers had first spotted me.

The snow had slowed to flurries. Patches of dark and starry sky became visible as clouds were clearing.

Four bodies stepped into view. Victorian winter clothes, hungry eyes, no mouths.

The carolers looked down at us from the street. They bent forward as one, glaring down into the sewer.

"Run!" David yelled, ushering us deeper.

We fled, hunched over, cement walls scraping our scalps and knuckles, into the dark. A line of not-red and not-purple lights guided our path.

18

I'D NEVER BEEN this far into the sewer before.

Since David had trouble fitting, and since the pipe seemed to go on forever, I'd always turned around after thirty or forty feet.

Now, as I navigated the cement pipe while avoiding touching the string of not-red and not-purple Christmas lights, I was acutely aware that each step took us further away from our only escape route. And that as tight as we were squeezed in here, there could be no quick escape.

But we couldn't turn back yet. My newfound desire propelled me—a similar flavor to why I'd decorated the house, but still evasive in exactly what it was. I wanted to kill the roots, cut the power to this perversion of our tacky lights contest, because...

Because nothing. I was still empty. I was just going along with my friends.

I followed David—and Harold followed me—deeper

into this downhill pipe. Somewhere ahead, past who-knows-how-many intersections and catch basins, the pipes emptied into a ditch that went past my house and down into the gulch.

"They're behind us!" Harold yelled in a panic.

David turned around, blinding me with the flashlight. "Who?"

"The carolers, dumbass!"

"How'd they get down here?"

Harold bumped into me. He shoved me into David. "Just run!"

I tried to pick up the pace, but keeping my feet from brushing the wire limited how fast I could scramble.

David ran awkwardly, bent forward with the back of his head bumping the pipe's ceiling, straddling the crawling wires on the cement floor.

I looked behind me, past Harold, to see the carolers walking at their slow pace. The not-red and not-purple lights at their feet barely lit their mouthless faces. The old man's cheek was still a mess of weird vertical vines from where Mrs. Perez had bumped into him.

That wasn't the part that confused me, though.

How could four adults be walking upright when my friends and I were hunched over? Were their legs wading through the cement like it was mud?

Harold pushed me. "Don't slow down."

As I turned back around, I bumped into David.

His boot brushed a not-purple lightbulb.

Instantly, the wire snapped up to tangle around his ankle, even as it continued its slithering journey uphill.

He tripped. I dodged around David but Harold crashed into him.

Fake snow, colored by the string lights, began to gather around them both.

I scrambled back to help. This wasn't the outer end of the light strands, like where they'd grabbed Harold's grandma. The wires were having trouble wrapping tight around my friends.

With the shears, I cut them free, but not before I got a clearer view of the carolers, now only twenty feet behind us in the pipe and walking perfectly upright.

If I looked at the pipe itself, then it was a four-foot diameter cement drain pipe. But if I looked at the carolers, in the periphery of my vision, the pipe opened as wide as infinity, gathering the night sky to make space for our pursuers.

David scrambled to his feet and crawled past me, panicking now. He raced down the pipe, kicking away the wire when it tried to grab him.

Harold and I hurried behind.

His light danced ahead of us and then dropped out of sight.

A moment later, I tumbled out of the pipe into a catch basin much too large.

19

I CAUGHT myself on the cement floor. The rough surface ripped my gloves and skinned my palms.

David was already on his feet. "What is that?"

This catch-basin was five times the size of the others. That couldn't be natural.

The pipe I'd just tumbled out from was one of two in the cement walls. Across the open space, another pipe opening continued downhill.

In the middle of the floor was a small crater. Cracks spiderwebbed out through the concrete. It reminded me of a bird hitting a glass window.

David aimed the flashlight at a chunk of *something* in the bottom of the crater.

It looked like a moldy and glittery eggplant. Its surface was gritty in a way that made me think it was a mineral, but it had waves and wrinkles that looked organic.

I stood up. The eggplant radiated that same desire I'd

felt from the carolers. It wanted to nestle its roots into what was empty so it could spread outward from there. "Don't touch it."

"No shit." David pointed the light away from the eggplant.

Before I could tell him to point it back, I saw what he was looking at. A tangle of roots like thin tentacles led from the eggplant in all directions. They were especially thick in a path toward the pipe we'd just come from.

Three feet from the source, this tangle of roots sprouted lightbulbs, which scraped along the cement floor. Another three feet and their moldy and glittery texture turned to green, rubbery wire. Right before they exited through the pipe, ready to join the invasion of Foothill Pines, the bulbs flashed to life, in not-red and not-purple.

Those were the light strands that snaked through the storm drain, that I'd fished out to decorate my unfinished house, that had spread like aggressive kudzu vines, that had taken Harold's grandma and David's mom and probably my parents and the rest of the neighborhood.

Even as we watched, the roots grew and the wires slithered.

Harold came running out from the pipe. He hit the floor and managed to stay standing. Weedkiller sloshed in the jug. "We gained some ground but the carolers are still coming." He took in the room around him and quickly aimed the spray wand at the eggplant. "That's the thing, right? The root we have to kill?"

"Do it." I relished the excitement of acting with

purpose. The more I let that desire fill me up—that desire to end this invasion—the less I felt that radiating *want* from the eggplant.

David interrupted us. He pointed at the ceiling. "Look."

A pea-sized hole.

I walked over next to my friend to see it from his angle.

Up through the hole, a layer of cement, then dirt, then pavement, then snow. Then a straight shot into the sky, through the thinning clouds, to the stars.

David said, "It was smaller when it crashed down."

"You think it's an alien?" Harold asked.

I was going to tell them to get on with it, but then David said, "Pump the sprayer" before I could. I felt the eggplant's hunger even more.

It was easier to let my friends do everything. I'd been in the background for the past year—I didn't need to do anything for this problem to be solved.

Harold set the jug down and pumped the handle.

David aimed the wand at the eggplant. He squeezed the trigger. Weedkiller splattered onto the moldy, glittery surface of the little lump. It sizzled.

Roots and wires kept on crawling out of the catch basin.

"It's not working." Harold pumped harder.

The caroler's song flooded into the room, a wordless version of "The Holly and the Ivy," echoing and repeating itself, bouncing off the cement walls.

It sent spikes of pain into my eardrums.

Harold bent over, clutching the sides of his head.

David whipped around to aim the spray wand at the pipe. He pointed the flashlight alongside it, but it only revealed the round, cement ceiling, stretching beyond our view. "Where are they?"

I barely heard him over the caroler's song.

Out from the dark corner behind David stepped the four carolers.

They loomed over my friend. Their faces strained with the rounds of their carol. The old bearded man's cheek still hung loose in thousands of vertical strands.

David took a careful step toward the pipe, trying to see inside, unaware of the threat behind him.

I yelled to my friend but the carolers' song grew louder.

They moved as one, knocking into him like a wave in an indifferent ocean.

He fell and they walked overtop.

They didn't care about him.

I was the empty one.

The carolers' eyes widened eagerly. They exuding that strange hunger I'd felt from them so much tonight, not to feed but for a place to expand their intentions.

Wires or vines or roots or whatever the hell they were went from the carolers' feet to the foreign eggplant. They were an appendage as much as the individual light strands.

They stepped toward me, in sync. I backed away until I felt the cement wall.

I raised the shears, aiming the opened blades at the carolers' chests.

Harold raced to my side. "Come on, we have to run."

"It's not dead yet!" If I abandoned my newfound goal to kill this thing, then what was left? Not Christmas. Not home. Maybe not even Mama and Dad.

"We're gonna be dead if we don't run." Harold pulled on my arm but I shook him off.

"We have to kill it."

"Look, David's up." Harold tried pulling me again. "Let's go!"

To David's credit, he didn't flee. He lugged the weed-killer, spraying the carolers as he circled them to join us.

Where the liquid splashed, their camouflage died. Wool pea coat and human skin alike flinched into masses of tiny roots.

But it didn't slow their methodical, unceasing advance.

"Why are they chasing us?" Harold took the tank from David and frantically pumped. "There's nothing empty down here."

"Self-preservation," David declared.

"Don't spray them," Harold shouted. "Spray the meteorite!"

While my friends panicked and tried to save us, I withdrew deeper into myself.

I was empty.

This foreign thing wanted empty spaces to grow out from. Houses would do but it really wanted me, a living empty host.

A burst of longing emanated from the eggplant so eager and clear that I saw its desire: its appendages filling my body cavity, sealing my mouth but bursting out from my eyes and nose and pores to grow forth from its ideal host and cover every square inch of Foothill Pines in Christmas, before moving on to the whole town, the county, the state. All it needed was empty, living soil in which to plant its roots.

"I'm sorry," I whispered.

David heard me but kept spraying. "What?"

The carolers were ten feet away now, bringing with them the master connection to the eggplant that would set its plan in motion.

"It's me. They followed me to Harold's house, then yours."

Harold shook his head. "No, it went to the Bakers' and Jones', too."

"The roots were spreading the whole time but the carolers have been following *me*. I can feel this desire from them, like when you're hungry and you want a whole pizza. You said it in your workshop. They want empty space. I'm empty."

David turned to me. "What are you saying?"

"I'm saying I'm empty and they've been following me and it's my fault. If you guys run, they won't follow you."

"We're not leaving you," Harold said.

David tried to assure me, "You're not empty."

Everything boiled over. "Then what am I? I used to have a family and we'd watch movies and go places and we'd do Christmas. Now what is there? Dad watches black-and-white TV shows and Mama doesn't do anything. I'm empty and that's the way everyone sees me."

"That's not true," David said.

"What did your parents say to me tonight? 'You shouldn't be out here on Christmas Eve.' 'Go call home since they must be worried because of last year.' All I am to anybody else is this empty shell that's supposed to have grief inside. They see me and only think of Erica and that makes me empty."

"The weirdos are getting closer," Harold said. "Keep spraying."

"You're not empty, dude." David turned back to soak the older woman's face in weedkiller.

"Yes I am and you proved it. On your workbench, the wires went for the empty microscope slides but ignored the full ones. And the carolers have been following me all night, walking right past other people. They just ran you over to get to me."

David stumbled over his next words. "That's not—that doesn't mean—maybe all that means is that they think you're empty."

"Why would they think that if it's not true?"

Harold took the spray wand from David and continued the defense.

David left him to it in order to hug me. "Maybe it's because you feel empty. But you're not."

The hug felt nice. It would have been nicer if I could really sink into it like I used to do with Dad and especially Mama. "What else am I supposed to feel? Do you know what it's like at my house? At least other grownups talk to me about Erica. Mama and Dad barely say anything at all. I was gonna show them the lights we put up so they'd see that I love Christmas so much. But that's obviously ruined."

"Dumbass," Harold said.

Even as we were about to die, his insult still hurt. "I know," I admitted. "I ruined a lot more than my Christmas. I'm sorry about your families. Maybe once the lights take me it'll give your families back."

"No, you're a dumbass because you said you're empty and the only thing about you is your dead sister."

"Hey," David shifted back into protective mode.

"The part that makes you a dumbass is you said that you want your parents to see how much you love Christmas. That's part of you, isn't it? Part of your personality. You're not empty. You like Christmas."

"Yeah," David agreed. "And pizza. You just said you like pizza when you're starving."

Harold sprayed the carolers as they approached, only a few feet now. "And you always pick Guile when we play Street Fighter. And Scorpion when we play Mortal Combat."

"That doesn't feel like much." I wanted to believe, but the events of the night were too much evidence against them.

"Listen to yourself," David said. "Christmas doesn't sound like much? You've been talking about your plans for this Christmas since Valentine's Day."

That was because I wanted my parents to be happy again. Except I did pick Christmas as the time to enact the plan. I could have picked any other day.

Maybe David was right. I tested out the words. "I'm not empty."

"Damn right," Harold said.

"I'm not empty!" I yelled louder.

The carolers slowed.

"I like pizza and Street Fighter and walking around the woods. And I fucking love Christmas!"

The carolers stopped. In the glow of the lights at their feet, they turned their heads this way and that, searching. They didn't sense me anymore.

Their song stuttered and lowered in volume.

"Come on," I said.

We slipped around the carolers. They didn't even notice.

I headed straight for the weird eggplant.

Moonlight now beamed down through the tiny hole in the ceiling. The clouds had cleared.

I imagined the original seed crashing down from the sky into our neighborhood, piercing the sidewalk to plant its roots down here beneath our Christmas preparations.

I didn't spend long imagining that. I opened the shears to drive a hole into the eggplant. Although the surface looked like a rock, it was as soft as a real eggplant.

I expected a shriek—it had done so much damage, it must be as alive as me. But it stayed quiet as a stone.

Harold warned us, "The carolers noticed that."

They turned around, walking faster than they had all night.

I jerked the shears back and forth, feeling the alien thing ripping as I widened the puncture wound. I pulled my weapon free. "Dump all the weedkiller in there."

Harold unscrewed the top, then he and David lifted it. A gallon of RoundUp GroundClear went right inside the eggplant.

In moments, its sparkly purple surface turned gray and dull. Brittleness spread outward, along its vines, snuffing out the lights.

For the first time in hours, silence returned as the carolers collapsed into dust.

No, not dust. Where before had stood the mouthless singers were now four knee-high Christmas decorations: dirty, porcelain, Victorian carolers with their mouths in little *Os*.

20

THE THREE OF us caught our breath.

"Is it over?" Harold asked.

"Yes," David declared.

We let the next question go unspoken. *Did we undo what was done?*

We crawled back up the pipe, over the dead and dissolving strands of lights.

When we reached the next catch basin, I said, "I'm climbing out here. I'll meet you guys above."

I climbed up and out from the rectangular curb drain.

"What do you see?" Harold asked.

I looked up Pine Whisper Way.

The neighborhood was now lit by moonlight and our regular tacky lights.

Lines and piles of gray dust littered the snowy yards, the streets, and the houses.

But all the invasive decorations were gone. No thick

jungle of lights up the middle of the street. No deformed blow molds and inflatables. The Jones' tree farm was a normal height again, although now covered in gray dust.

"It's just the neighborhood again," I said.

On the empty house across the street, my lights shone bright. I liked them.

"Is anyone outside?" David asked.

Across the street from Harold's house, a toppled wire reindeer decoration rose to its feet.

Mr. Brinks stood up behind it, making sure he'd balanced it properly. He brushed off his knees, then hugged his chest and looked around.

"Mr. Brinks!" I shouted. "He's okay."

"Grandma!" Harold yelled hopefully, and then he and David were hurrying back through the snowmelt drains, back to the pipe they could fit through.

I rubbed my shoulders. Maria still had my coat.

Suddenly, I was yanked into the air and squeezed. I kicked once until I recognized Dad's embrace.

"Douglas!" Mama hugged me from behind.

Now that I was safe, I could recognize how exhausted I was. Every muscle in my body was shot. My fingers were numb with cold even through my tattered gloves. My palms stung from the scrapes.

I pressed my cheek against Dad's. "I was scared the lights got you." His rough stubble was comforting. He only had it in the evenings, when he was getting us ready for bed.

Dad set me down and crouched to look me in the eyes. "Why in the world did you sneak out?"

"We can scold him later." Mama hugged my head against her belly. Her ski jacket was cool and slick. "We should get home. We don't know if it's safe yet."

"Did you see the lights?" I asked.

"I'm not sure what happened," Dad said. "We came out to look for you but the Wellington's train up on the corner derailed. It ran us over."

"We saw the lights," Mama told me. "That train came barreling down the hill right through them. It was as big as a real locomotive."

"And I swear to God," Dad said, "Snoopy was riding on top like some kind of hellhound."

"Don't scare him," Mama said.

"I was in it, too."

Mama let out a sob and held me more tightly.

Dad exhaled. "Things got bright and confusing. I don't know what was happening. Then we heard you yelling about Christmas and pizza and we were back on the street." He hugged me again. "I was so scared for you. Don't you ever run off again."

Up the hill, I saw Mr. Perez and Maria stagger out from the behind the Jones' normal-sized tree farm. David and Mrs. Perez ran down the street to pull their family into an embrace.

"What happened to them?" Dad asked. His grip on my shoulder tightened. "Are your friends okay? Where's the other one? The one you don't like."

It surprised me that he remembered me complaining about Harold. I didn't think he'd been listening. "We're all okay," I said.

Harold came running down the hill behind the Perez family. He ignored them and Mr. Brink to run into his open front door.

I heard his joyful cry from outside. "Grandma!"

We'd seen her eyeball and her mouth in separate lightbulbs. How could killing the alien plant bring her back?

Maybe what we'd seen had been copies made after the vines had grabbed her. Or maybe it was what David had promised Harold: a Christmas miracle.

Mama got stiff. She tugged on Dad's coat. "We need to go *now*."

"What's wrong?" Dad pushed us behind him, scanning for danger.

"That new construction." She pointed to my house—the one I'd decorated. My little display of porch lights and the patched-up inflatable Mickey Mouse were a lone bright spot in this new section of Foothill Pines. "Those lights don't belong. It's not over."

"Those are mine," I quickly said. "I put them up before everything happened. I did it for you guys."

This wasn't the big reveal I'd wanted.

Dad's shoulders relaxed. He stepped back beside me. "You did all that? Where'd you get the lights?"

"They're nice," Mama said. "Why'd you'd do it, though?"

I knew my answer. I'd told David and Harold. I'd

screamed it at the carolers. But for all the courage that had taken, I still struggled to say the words now.

I was showing Mama and Dad my light display, like I'd been planning for a month. It was Christmas Eve, the night I'd been looking forward to all year.

All I had to do was tell them.

I reached out and held their hands—Mama on the left, Dad on the right. "Because I love Christmas, Mama."

She pulled me close. "Me, too."

WHY I WROTE THIS BOOK

I FUCKING LOVE CHRISTMAS.

- Ben Farthing, November 2023

ARE YOU A STRANGE READER?

Hello Strange Reader,

Stephen King has "Constant Readers." But you just read a book about people getting turned into Christmas decorations, so I figure you'll happily wear the title of "Strange Reader."

I'd like to invite you to visit my website where you'll find some exclusive bonus material for 'I Found Christmas Lights Slithering Up My Street.'

I'll ask you for your email address so you can be part of my "Strange Reader Newsletter," but you're welcome to unsubscribe at any time.

To access the bonus content, scan this QR code with your phone's camera app:

IT WAITS ON THE TOP FLOOR

The tower appeared overnight, but it wants to keep you forever.

"If you like dark, twisted, raise-the-hair-on-the-back-of-your-neck horror, you can't go wrong with this book!" - Booknerdia

Thursday night, it was a dirt lot.

Friday morning, it was a 60-story skyscraper.

A tech billionaire wants the building's secrets for herself. She hires a team to reverse-engineer the overnight construction. But she knows more than she's letting on.

A curious 9-year-old decides there's treasure inside, and goes exploring. His terrified dad chases close behind. Inside, the facade of an empty office building is quickly shattered. Ghostly figures stalk the explorers. The walls themselves are hungry. And something is waiting on the top floor.

It Waits On the Top Floor is the first book in the *Horror Lurks Beneath* trilogy. It's available as an ebook, paperback, and audiobook.

THE PIPER'S GRAVEYARD

A mysterious evil haunts a small town's radio waves.

★★★★★ *"A scary atmosphere and great characters." Goodreads Review.*

Cessy returns home to search for her missing sister.

She finds a half-abandoned town under siege by unexplainable threats: Attics and crawlspaces stretch into endless tunnels. Corpses turn up riddled with holes—holes that slither through flesh like insectile parasites. It all leads deep into the abandoned coal mine.

Cessy's sister disappeared while investigating the vengeful voice on the radio. To find her, Cessy will have to unravel the dark mystery wriggling up from the coal mine.

The Piper's Graveyard is available as an ebook, paperback, and audiobook.

ABOUT THE AUTHOR

Ben Farthing writes supernatural horror. He lives with his wife and children near Richmond, Virginia. Follow him on Facebook, Instagram, and TikTok.